CHAPTER I

HER wedding ring was a broad platinum band. Next to it an engagement ring, very old, very beautiful, a hoop of pearls glistening like frozen tears, pure, costly, and as unblemished as each of the brides who down the centuries had known the honour of being the chosen bride of the reigning Marqués de Drach. "The Ring of Chastity," she had heard it whispered, "demands of its wearer a matching purity. If any male member of the family should bestow its bounty upon one less worthy then the vengeance of the dragon will be aroused!" *Todo o nada*! All or nothing! The motto of the family of Drach was as terse and uncompromising as its menfolk.

"*Con su permiso*?" A deep masculine voice startled her into the present, asking if she minded his lighting one of the thin black cigars he favoured. For a second her startled eyes reflected aloofness, a reluctance to associate with strangers, then her cheeks flared brilliant pink as she stammered a reply to her husband of one hour: "Of course not ... please do ...!"

The main salon of the Casa was seething with guests, all expensively dressed, the dark-eyed, raven-haired women whispering discreetly behind bejewelled hands, their only faintly less curious husbands trying without success to quell the interest of their gossiping wives.

"I think the time has come for us to mingle." Francisco slipped a cool hand beneath her elbow and began

5

guiding her towards the nearest group of guests. Hazel stiffened; for an hour she had suffered the agony of introductions, weathering a battery of piercing eyes as couple after couple had filed past to offer their congratulations and best wishes. But she had not been deceived. The prettily phrased words had held a hollow ring and the accompanying smiles a gathering of frost. She was an impostor, they were all very well aware. How could it be otherwise when Francisco Calvente y Formentor, Marqués de Drach, had betrayed on so many occasions his dislike and distrust of women – particularly Englishwomen?

Guided by his determined hand she moved towards the ranks of what she felt were her enemies. Beneath the delicate lace of her wedding gown her heart lurched with fear, but her face reflected a quality of serenity that enabled him to relax fractionally his grip upon her arm. She felt slight amusement at the thought that he, too, might be nervous – no, not nervous, such a word was alien to his character. Disturbed? Yes, that better described the present state of mind of the imperturbable Marqués. From somewhere, she found enough composure to chat amiably as they circulated amongst the guests. The champagne helped, and mercifully there was always a servant at hand to replenish her glass whenever the golden supply of liquid courage threatened to run dry. Then after an interminable interval, it was time to retire to the dining salon where great lengths of table covered with cloths of finest silk damask, set with glittering crystal, elegant silver, and breathtaking flower arrangements awaited the serving of the wedding luncheon.

This part she found easier. Perhaps it was because the champagne she was unused to had numbed her senses, or then again it might have been the fact that Francisco, now completely relaxed, had ceased silently demanding that she portray the dignity expected of her new station – demands her perceptive impulses had reacted to instinctively – and was now in such a softened mood his mouth was curved into lines of indulgence. She had pleased him! The worst was now over and shortly she would be allowed to return into the obscurity from whence she came ...

Not all of the guests were distant. Don Garcia, Francisco's uncle, sat on her right, and the attentions of the elderly *hidalgo* whose shrewd eyes kindled with kindness whenever they met hers soothed the frightened thudding of her heart into a less disturbing beat. She was absently forking the giant shrimps on her plate through a piquant lobster sauce when his concerned voice questioned, "The *langostinos* are not to your taste, *cara*?" The fork clattered from nerveless fingers, causing raised eyebrows and supercilious smiles from those near enough to notice. Immediately, Francisco's attention swung towards her, his face bearing the beginnings of a frown, but his uncle repaired the damage he had unwittingly caused by smoothly changing the subject.

"By the way, Francisco, why is the little Carmen not present on this most important occasion? One would imagine her eager to witness the marriage between her uncle and her dear English friend. The arrangement has made her ecstatically happy, I believe?"

A rippled murmur ran through the assembly. *Arrangement* was perhaps not the wisest choice of word,

and the quick thinning of his lips betrayed Don Garcia's own inward annoyance.

Francisco's clipped reply brought a flush of indignation to Hazel's cheeks. "Carmen's penchant for bad behaviour has resulted in my once more having to resort to punishment," he enlightened with distaste. "This morning I was left no choice but to banish her to her room for the rest of today so that she might perhaps begin to realise that explanations, however glibly given, will not be accepted as excuses for disobedience."

Hazel almost cried out. It took great effort of will not to round upon the arbitrary Marqués and accuse him of coldblooded cruelty to the sensitive, bewildered child so recently bereaved of both parents. Parents whose greatest mistake in seven years of parenthood had been their misguided choice of guardian for their only child. Only the warning signal flashed to her by Don Garcia restrained the impulse to commit the unforgivable sin of contradicting her husband in front of his guests.

As if he sensed her rebellion, Francisco's glance flickered over her, then, with an indifferent shrug, he dismissed the subject of his niece and turned to his companion to continue their interrupted conversation. Indignation forced a lump to Hazel's throat, making even pretence of eating an impossibility. The child had been wildly delighted at the prospect of taking part in the ceremony. For days she had talked of little else but the duties she would be called upon to perform, little things Hazel had invented deliberately so that her presence in the church would seem of outstanding importance: the positioning of the heavy lace bridal

8

train, the care of the pearl rosary which was to have been placed in the child's keeping while the actual vows were being taken, the handkerchief she was to have hidden in readiness in case – just in case – Hazel was tempted to sneeze. And the bridesmaid's dress, the delicate pale pink concoction, frilled and beribboned enough to delight any child, which was now hanging in the wardrobe of Carmen's room, a tormenting reminder of what might have been ...

After lunch, their guests began taking their leave. "The honeymoon has been postponed because of pressure of work," Francisco smoothly informed them as, thanking them for their presence, he sped them on their way. "Doubtless, later in the year, we will agree upon a place and a date." By his side she stood dignified and calm, accepting the parting good wishes and ignoring the pitying looks that communicated plainly their owners' doubts of her ever having her wishes consulted upon any matter, however small.

Don Garcia was last to make his goodbyes. His car and chauffeur were waiting at the front of the house, but he hesitated when just as he was leaving he heard Francisco inform his bride with formal politeness, "For the next few hours I shall be in my study catching up on some work. Please see that I am not disturbed." Her cool word of acknowledgement caused Don Garcia's eyebrows to rise and when his nephew's footsteps began retreating across the marble floor he dismissed his chauffeur and moved back inside the hall of the casa. Hazel was still standing where Francisco had left her, a slight, lonely figure, her bent head caught by sun rays spearing through the windows to form a nimbus around

her hair, transforming it with the sheen of rich chestnut. In her pure white dress, simple as a habit, she reminded him of a novice preparing to be sacrificed upon the altar of duty.

"Child!" He strode towards her, compassion stirring in his heart. With a stifled gasp she looked up, but did not flinch from the sagacity of his wise old eyes. "Shall we walk together in the garden?" he offered, extending his arm with the gallantry of an ancient conquistador. Mist slowly dispersing from her eyes to reveal the beginning of a sparkle made him think of sunlight imprisoned in amber.

"I'd like that very much, Don Garcia," she trembled, on the brink of a smile.

They sauntered through gardens to the rear of the casa, passing sunken rose gardens and sloping, finely-shaven lawns until they reached less cultivated ground, then they halted on the edge of sheer cliff, looking down upon ragged-edged boulders tracing a way down to a minute cove where golden sand was lapped by sea blue as a madonna's cloak. With unspoken agreement they sat down upon a seat carefully positioned many years before by someone with mind aesthetically attuned to surrounding beauty. She had discarded her headdress and veil, and her lace gown with its prim collar, tight-fitting sleeves and billowing skirt fitted perfectly into a landscape dominated by the rubble-work pile of natural stone that formed the Casa de Drach.

Following her backward glance, Don Garcia waved a languid hand in its direction and twinkled, "Castle of the Dragon, I believe, is the correct English translation.

Were you not just a little apprehensive, my dear, at the thought of being joined in matrimony to a man whose enemies have been known to refer to him as the 'reigning monster'?" He was prepared for a laughing response, but when her cheeks drained of colour and lashes swept down too late to hide a glint of fear, he cursed inwardly and tried to make light of his words.

"My late sister, Francisco's mother, was often teased in this vein. I've often suspected that the men of the Drach family enjoy the reputation their name suggests, and naturally their dark good looks, together with an inherited tendency for brooding passion, hardly detracts from the image. All through the centuries, however, their womenfolk have remained faithful and loving. Not one broken or unhappy marriage has been recorded, hence the foundation for my assertion that these women were privileged to see a side of the men of Drach known to only a very few. Indeed, this was proved to me by my sister when once she defended her husband's seeming abruptness. In my indignation I had resorted to abuse and referred to him as 'the beast', only to be rebuked: 'The blame lies with you, Garcia, for prodding him into anger. The mighty cannot be tamed by force, only by guile, and only he who accepts that fact will know the pleasure of hearing a dragon's purr."

Hazel had to smile; the picture he painted of a purring Francisco was a fantasy too remote to be taken seriously. "Your sister was obviously very much in love, Tio, so her idealism can be understood and therefore excused." An unhappy silence followed words which both recognized as a confession, the confession

of a bride unloving and unloved. Don Garcia's sagging shoulders indicated deep concern, which was intensified when he glimpsed two large single tears caught and held in a tangle of tawny lashes.

"I am too old to feel curiosity, *cara*, but if talking will help then I am willing to listen?"

Her sideways glance dislodged the tears which she allowed to trickle unchecked down her cheeks. For searching, uncertain minutes she held his look, delving deep into his heart, and when he did not flinch from the scrutiny she forced out the whispered admission, "I've made a terrible mistake, Tio Garcia, but for Carmen's sake I must see it through to the end!"

"Begin at the beginning," he commanded gently.

At first she faltered, searching for words, then with her eyes fixed on the gentle swell of ocean she began unfolding the series of events leading up to her present situation.

"I suppose it all began in Newcastle," she surprised him by beginning. "I worked there, in a solicitor's office, right opposite a travel agency whose windows were always bright with posters showing golden beaches, blue skies, and happy, laughing people." He noted the wistful reference to happiness and was not surprised to hear her sigh before going on. "It was the posters that made me decide. I lived most of my life with my grandmother – my parents died when I was very small and she looked after me right up until she died six months ago."

This explained more than she knew to the astute old man. Several times he had tried to put his finger on the difference he sensed lay between her and the young

English girls who abounded on the beaches of the more populated parts of the island, but now it was understandable why she should appeal to him as having been laid up in lavender . . . "Typing contracts and wills day after day can be boring, so as a diversion I used to go across to the travel agency each lunchtime to browse through their literature and to observe and envy the clients who found it hard to decide which place to choose. That was a difficulty I never had to face. From the very first, Majorca was my ideal, and although I never imagined myself being able to afford a visit, I spent hours choosing the resort and the hotel I preferred. Then," her voice hushed as she relived the memory, "I learned of the money left to me by my grandmother – a small amount by your standards" – she added hastily, "but sufficient for me to afford to turn a dream into reality."

"Our island has not disappointed you, I hope?" he prompted when she lapsed into silence.

"No, not the island," Hazel hesitated, colouring slightly, "but some of the men at the hotel . . ."

He nodded. "But of course," he countered with raised eyebrows, "what else did you expect? A young girl alone on an island made for romance – what man could resist such a challenge?"

"I hid from them," she confessed, full of awkward shyness. "I've had no experience of men – except for elderly solicitors – so each day after breakfast I took a bus far into the hills to seek a stretch of beach where I could spend the day alone."

"Ah!" he snapped his fingers as light dawned, "that explains Carmen's fanciful references to finding treasure

on the beach! You are the one who spent hours playing with the child, the one who brightened her days so much that she began racing through her breakfast in order to get down to the beach, whereas before she had had to be forced into accompanying one of the long-suffering servants!"

"I had no idea the beach was private," she stammered. "At first it seemed deserted and ... and ..."

"Safe?" he suggested dryly.

"Perhaps," she sighed.

Don Garcia was perturbed. Hazel's natural timidity should have resulted in instinctive withdrawal from his nephew's bitter arrogance; how then had the two most unlikely candidates for matrimony bridged the gulf of opposing personalities?

As if reading his mind, she supplied the answer. "One day, the Marqués discovered our secret. He was on his way for a swim when he heard us laughing. At first, I thought he seemed angry to find his niece playing with a total stranger, a trespasser, but after a few terse questions he allowed me to stay. Then a few days later he instructed Carmen to invite me up to the Casa for lunch ..." He sensed from her expression that she was reliving a traumatic experience, but even he, cushioned as he was against his nephew's often startling actions, was shattered when she admitted, "That same day he offered me a job. A beautiful home, luxury, and a life-time of security, he said, in return for companionship for Carmen and," her throat worked as she choked on the words, "a business marriage to be contracted solely to allay the suspicions of gossiping neighbours ..."

Don Garcia's breath hissed furiously through

clenched teeth. "*Madre de Dios!*" he exclaimed in a whisper, "I would not have believed even Francisco capable of such utter insensitivity!" When she flinched his concern deepened. She was such a child, the mere thought of her being bound for life by a promise which should never have been sought outraged and confounded him. "Why on earth did you accept such a proposal?" he probed with unthinking haste. "Why didn't you decline the coldblooded offer in words which would have left Francisco in no doubt of the distaste you must have felt?"

Her cheeks were afire when she stammered a confused explanation. "I was lonely . . . Carmen needed me, and I know only too well the yearning for love and understanding. And besides," her voice dropped to a whisper as if she felt ashamed to admit such lack of independence, "the silence can be pretty deafening for a woman alone . . ."

CHAPTER II

WHEN the still puzzled, only half convinced Don Garcia finally left, Hazel went up to her room. Although she knew Francisco was still in his study her heart jerked as she turned the knob and stepped into the bridal suite. "Our rooms must adjoin," he had decreed, sweeping aside her suggestion that she should remain near Carmen in case the child should awaken during the night. "It is a necessary part of the deception; I will not tolerate gossiping servants!" She tiptoed inside, feeling an interloper, loath even to touch the many costly heirlooms bequeathed by her predecessors to future brides. Every room in the Casa was overwhelmingly luxurious, but the vividly painted ceilings, jewel-toned tapestries and dark carved wooden panelling of the main rooms were usurped in the bridal suite by a colour scheme predominantly ivory, gilt and pearl. Ivory satin draped the windows and cascaded from a gilt coronet placed high above the bed, falling like a veil to screen its occupant in mystery. Fragile gilt chairs, silk-embroidered to match the bed covers, added colour so muted it blended into the background with less impact than a shadow. Mirrors of every shape hung around the walls, all with frames encrusted with tiny seed pearls. Pearl-ornamented combs and brushes scattered the dressing table, together with jewel boxes, powder bowls and perfume bottles – presents from husbands anxious to uphold family tradition by match-

ing flawlessness with innocence, bestowing purity upon the chaste . . .

Hazel went into the bathroom to take a shower. The water, deliciously cool, needled her alive and chased the dejected droop from her shoulders. Slowly her spirits revived. Things might not be so bad, she consoled herself as she towelled dry. Francisco had promised her security and a luxurious way of life far removed from anything she had ever known, and up until now his promises had all been kept. Only yesterday she had been summoned to his study and in the presence of his solicitor had watched him scrawl his signature on a marriage settlement generous enough to ensure her financial security for the rest of her life.

She wandered back into the bedroom and sat at the dressing table to stare thoughtfully at her mirrored reflection. How little he was to receive from the arrangement! His wealth could have bought him a poised, assured hostess, an expert conversationalist, faultless in face and figure. Remembering the nickname her school friends had given her, her eyes clouded and her small pointed features became bleak. Hazel Brown – *Nutbrown*! The teasing name had always struck her as unkind. Brown eyes, revealed golden only when afire with happiness or light, brown hair streaked here and there chestnut red, and a *brown* personality, she mocked in self-disgust, meek, timid, and so boringly *ordinary*! Quickly she averted her eyes and jumped to her feet. Self-pity would get her nowhere; the least she could do was see that Francisco received some value for money, and the only way to do that was to carry out exceptionally well the job she was being paid to do.

In a matter of seconds she had pulled on a sleeveless cotton dress, green as young shoots, and after pushing her bare feet into thonged sandals she padded outside and along the corridor to Carmen's room. She hesitated outside the door. Carmen, like herself, hated wasting time in siesta, but the little one's crying bout could have exhausted her and Hazel had no wish to rouse her from sleep. Noiselessly, she pushed open the door and crept towards the bed, which was shrouded in dimness caused by shuttered windows. She hardly breathed as she peeped across the foot, but instinct must have warned Carmen she was not alone, because she lifted her head from the pillow and quavered: "Who's there?"

"Can't you guess?" Hazel teased, a bright smile hiding the heartache she felt at the sight of Carmen's quivering mouth and tear-swollen eyes.

"Hazel! Hazel!" the child screamed, lifting her arms in an impulsive demand for comfort.

"Oh, poor baby!" Hazel gathered Carmen's gulp-racked frame in loving arms. "Don't cry any more, sweetheart, I'm here now and I'm staying for good – or for as long as you need me."

"Then that will be for ever and ever! Promise, Hazel, promise . . .?" Carmen's thin arms urged with a love that had its true strength been demonstrated, would have cracked Hazel's slender frame in half.

"Yes, yes, I promise," she laughed, trying to extricate herself from the demanding clutch. Firmly she discouraged further emotion by decreeing, "Your most important need at the moment is a wash. Come on, out of bed with you, and while you're deciding upon a dress I'll turn on the shower. Quickly now,

there's not much time left before dinner!" Not without qualms of conscience, she led Carmen on tiptoe past the study door. Once they reached the garden their footsteps quickened until by the time they had reached the beach their breathing was jerky and they were trembling as if they had weathered the *solano*, the sultry wind peasants referred to as "dragon's breath".

"He'll be furious when he finds out we have disobeyed him," Carmen informed her with the calm panache of one who has often experienced wrath.

"Nonsense!" Hazel tried to laugh, but her heart sank. Carmen was inclined to be precocious – the result of always having mixed with grown-ups rather than children – to the extent that sometimes Hazel felt she was conversing with another adult, one more sophisticated and worldly than herself. "Your uncle was very angry with you when he banished you to your room, but I'm sure he will have relented by now. Even he must realize that missing the wedding service was punishment enough."

That "*even he*" was a mistake she would have retracted the moment it was said, and the faint hope that Carmen might have missed the emphasis flickered into extinction when the child seized upon it with relish. "Tio Francisco is a monster, you know," she told an appalled Hazel. "I heard my mother say so to my father once." The small earnest face grew sad as she recalled her parents, and Hazel had not the heart to chastise her when with a prim censure that sat oddly upon her childish features Carmen repeated more overheard conversation. "My mother was betrothed to Tio

Francisco, but she married my father instead, which made Tío so angry he would not allow him to continue working in the business nor even to pay a visit. It was wrong that the elder brother should have so much and the younger so little, my mother said, so she insisted upon my father approaching Tío just once more, because we had very little money and my father could not find work as his knowledge was all of the business and was very spesh . . . spesh . . ."

"Specialized?" Hazel offered faintly.

"Yes, just as you say!" Carmen nodded triumphantly. "It means secret, I think, because when my mother urged him to contact someone who would have given a lot of money for information about the business he refused, saying he could not give away family secrets, not even to spite Tío . . . It was then that my mother called Tío a monster!"

"Hush!" Hazel clapped her hand over Carmen's mouth to still further confidences. She did not want to know another thing about the vendetta that had existed between the two brothers, because what little she had learnt had left her feeling burnt up with anger against parents who could burden a child with their troubles, however unthinkingly, and against the man who was not above allowing hatred of his brother and the woman who had spurned him to colour his attitude towards their orphaned child. Why he had been chosen as her guardian was a mystery – as big a mystery as the man himself who, for all his distaste of the situation, had accepted such a responsibility.

For the next hour they occupied themselves by building sand castles and when that palled they played

quoits on the smooth stretch of beach. She had not allowed Carmen to become over-excited, but pleasurable activity shared with a companion who could shed years at will resulted in her voice rising shrill and penetrating as they returned to the *casa*. Carmen stumbled as she entered the hall, and the ball she was holding flew from her hands to bounce noisily across the marble floor. Her shriek of laughter as she joyfully chased it was piercing enough to have reached the alabaster ears of the cherubs reclining in most unchildlike attitudes upon the magnificent ceiling and seemed even to raise the painted eyebrows of the stern-faced men and their beautiful wives whose portraits lined the vast museum-like hall. Certainly, it must have penetrated the massive door of hand-carved wood leading into Francisco's study, because it was thrown open by his impatient hand, and when he recognized the culprit his features set with frowning displeasure.

"Carmen!" She halted in her tracks. "Why aren't you in your room?"

Her chin took on an impish tilt, but before she could answer Hazel intervened; the child was not usually impudent, but she had inherited enough of her uncle's temperament to give a pert answer if pushed. "It was my idea, Francisco," she stumbled over the name he had insisted she should use. "It's not good for the child to be alone in a stuffy room, so I decided . . ."

"*You* decided?" The icy query was so insultingly stressed she was rendered dumb. His hard look raked her hot, miserable face before glancing across to Carmen. "Leave us, *aprisa*!" he commanded, his tone communicating unmistakably the threat of retribution. When

Carmen's footsteps scampered out of earshot his attention was trained once more upon Hazel. "Before this day is much older we must reach an understanding, you and I," he directed coldly across her bent head. "I should like to see you here in my study half an hour before dinner, so that I may instruct you further in the manner in which any future orders of mine are to be carried out."

The study door closed, leaving her staring wide-eyed and apprehensive around the hall which now seemed filled with silent laughter. Fearfully, her glance was drawn along the line of sombre portraits, then quickly she looked away. It could have been a trick of light, but each proud profile seemed to have assumed an attitude of scorn, the resurrected eyes glinting their contempt of the imposter in their midst. Fighting a wave of trembling she forced herself to walk past them until she reached the staircase where, with her feet on the first step, she braved a second look. Dark shadows were fingering huge tapestries depicting a youthful warrior, with lance poised, astride a thoroughbred horse whose slender legs pranced just out of range of the jaws of a fire-breathing dragon. As was to be expected, there was a maiden in distress cowering nearby, her worshipping eyes showering adoration upon her would-be deliverer. She was represented as a pearl in the Drach family *escudo*, a symbol of the beauty and purity they held so dear, and the dragon was the monster temper, which curse had bedevilled Drach men throughout the ages. Hazel shivered, recalling Francisco's leashed anger. The curse still flourished – but how ardently, and with what amount of strength was it controlled?

She began ascending the stairs with weary, despondant steps, but even the minimal amount of draught she caused was sufficient to set off the tinkling of bells. A corner of her mouth lifted and she hesitated, delighted as always by the sound. The wrought iron balustrade was fashioned into ears of wheat so delicately formed that the slightest passage of air was enough to set them swaying. Tree trunks of slender iron gave support where it was needed, but their leaves and branches combined artistry with strength. The tinkling came from bells hung about the necks of goats by finely wrought ribbons, and even the shepherd's crooks responded with a satisfying sway to the force of a well-aimed breath. To Hazel, the staircase was a source of beauty and joy, it spoke to her in a language of hope, proving by its very existence that the arrogant and feared Drach family betrayed by its love of beauty a strain of deep sensitivity. As she ran the rest of the way upstairs the joyous carillon that accompanied her found an echo in a heart full of sudden happiness.

She took a long time deciding which dress to wear for dinner that evening. Her choice was limited because her grandmother's legacy had not stretched far enough to allow for more than two evening dresses, but both were new and the novelty of owning even one such extravagant luxury still possessed her. After much deliberation she discarded green cotton in favour of a bronze velvet with long, tight-fitting sleeves ending in a point below her wrist. Its uncluttered lines hugged her slim body, flattering her tiny waist and outlining the thrust of small breasts. An embroidered girdle hanging loosely around her waist was its only decoration, and the

result was simplicity with a medieval quality that blended well with her surroundings. She would need more clothes, Francisco had informed her with such detachment that they might have been discussing the replacement of servants' uniforms – even now the bored edge of his remark rankled enough to set her cheeks afire. She sat down with cooling hands pressed to her face and watched with a mixture of impatience and terror the hands of the clock creeping slowly forward, then, at the time stipulated, she began making her way downstairs to present herself in his study.

He was standing lance-straight in front of a marble fireplace that rose sheer from the floor to ceiling, yet he did not seem dominated. Rather he seemed part of it, dignified, aristocratic, unyielding. Hazel shivered and moved forward, responding to commanding eyes so dark and thickly fringed that they recalled to mind reeded pools, shaded with mystery. His voice projected cold, it flicked steel-tipped indifference into even conventional greeting. "*Buenas tardes,* your punctuality pleases me. I deplore the vanity of most of your sex who suffer from the delusion that a man's interest becomes more marked the longer he is kept waiting." One black eyebrow rose questioningly when she smiled wryly.

"As a child I was never permitted the indulgence of even the small sin of vanity, so you are quite safe, I would never presume an interest where I know interest cannot exist."

"Cannot?" He moved forward, curiosity momentarily replacing aloofness, to study her upturned face, and immediately she was disarmed. For the first time she held his complete attention and as he perused her softly

flushed cheeks and uncertain mouth the experience wreaked havoc in her heart. A log hissed and collapsed into the heart of the fire, sending out a flare of vivid orange light. For the second she was caught within its range her hair took on glorious life, and a quickly indrawn breath evidenced his surprise as flame was held prisoner in eyes of deepest amber, lending to them a rare beauty. Grudgingly, when the flame had died, he was moved to admit, "You do yourself an injustice, *mia cara*. Yours is not an obvious beauty, but a man willing to search in depth would, I'm sure, find much to interest him."

She flinched from the hint of condescension in his tone. His assessment was so unfeelingly blunt it could have come only from one completely indifferent to the inflicting of pain. To him, she was too much of a nonentity to merit even the small effort of a compliment. The knowledge stung – stung so much that she had to bite hard to steady her trembling bottom lip.

Glasses clinked upon a silver salver as Francisco poured out drinks. Without asking her preference, he handed her a fluted glass containing golden wine and indicated that she should drink. She was perched on the edge of a chair and when he sat down opposite and began studying her she took a nervous gulp, then almost choked as the very dry sherry bit into the back of her throat. "*Por mi vida*! Have you so little respect for wine that you gulp it down like *limonada*?" he scolded even as he thrust a crisp handkerchief into her fist. He waited unsympathetically until her spasm of coughing was under control, then offered dryly, "It would appear there are now two children resident in the Casa. I had

not realized how very immature you are, but still," he stared thoughtfully into his glass like a seer probing the future, "perhaps it is not such a bad thing. When I employed you to entertain Carmen and to keep her out of my way was I conscious that the child's real need was for companionship of her own age, and yet I was not prepared to have the Casa overrun by unruly brats. Once you accept that my orders are to be obeyed *implicitly* you should be able to command from Carmen the modicum of respect due to an older, more responsible playmate," he suddenly mocked.

Carefully, Hazel set down her glass; his galling amusement had roused a dignity she had not known she possessed. His eyes were upon her hands clenched tightly on her lap, so he missed the sparkle of humiliated tears and heard only a small cool voice as she charged, "It's gratifying to discover you have a sense of humour, *señor*, even if its cruel and somewhat peculiar quality causes amusement only to yourself. You may be right in implying that I have the mind of a child, but at least Carmen will never suffer from my hands the sophisticated type of torture which allowed you to snatch from the child's reach a long-awaited treat as punishment for what was really a very small misdemeanour." She faltered when his head snapped up, temper showing in an arrogant flare of nostrils.

"You call deliberate disobedience a small misdemeanour?" he clipped.

"She was excited because she had waited so long for the wedding day to arrive," Hazel stammered. "To a child a week can seem like a year when a treat is in store, and she really did forget in her excitement that

you had forbidden her to waken me early. And it wasn't as if I was asleep . . ."

"Enough !" Black eyes glittered angry displeasure as he waved away her flow of nervous excuses. He stood up, evidently determined to end the conversation, but courage welled up and enabled her to spurt out the words. "Why don't you try making friends with Carmen ? She's such a lonely little scrap, she misses her parents more than you seem to realize. Couldn't you . . ." she gulped back the lump of fear that suddenly threatened to choke her, "couldn't you try to take the place of her father – your brother – after all, you must feel some affection for the child you've taken into care . . ."

He had melted into the shadows, so she could not read the expresssion on his face, but something about his tall, lean outline warned her that she had over-stepped the boundary of what was allowed to be said to the aloof Marqués. In spite of the glowing fire the room felt hung with chill, she shivered, then jerked like a startled fawn when his voice lashed out of the darkness. "The child is here on sufferance, not out of any feeling of affection but simply to appease a prick of conscience." He hesitated fractionally, then, with such austere detachment he could have been voicing a platitude, he concluded, "I'm sure you'll agree that it was the least I could do, considering I was responsible for the death of her parents !"

CHAPTER III

WHEN Hazel received a letter from the hotel informing her that some small items she had left behind were awaiting collection, Tio Garcia put his car and himself at her disposal. The resort where she had stayed was on the east side of the island, about two hours' slow drive through sloping, tree-lined roads leading downwards from hills where the Casa brooded in solitary isolation. As they neared civilization villas began appearing, pink and white-washed walls, gaily-tiled roofs, the inevitable swimming pools of sea-blue tiles set amidst pocket-sized gardens, each being tended by the languid but loving hands of old Spanish gardeners who saluted with a wide grin and a courteous wave everyone who passed. Carmen was thrilled to be included in the outing and she and Tio Garcia chatted non-stop until the chauffeur drove up the small palm-lined drive leading to the front of the hotel. They remained in the car while she collected her parcel, and she was just about to rejoin them when a voice hailed her in such familiar terms she halted in her tracks.

"*Nut-brown*! Hazel! Is it really you?"

"Catryn Wade?" Hazel chanced uncertainly, catching a fleeting resemblance to a school friend in the beautiful face of the girl who stood beaming down at her.

"In the flesh!" she nodded so vehemently that her hair fell like a mimosa curtain across her cheeks.

Impatiently, she swept it back to allow brilliant blue eyes full access to Hazel's slight figure. "You haven't changed, Nut-brown, I'd have known your wistful little face anywhere!"

Hazel's heart sank. Catryn had not changed either, certainly the years had added to an ever-present beauty, but her mouth still retained the small cruel quirk which so often in the past had preceded a string of taunts that had turned Hazel's schooldays into periods of misery.

"I must rush, Catryn," she mumbled, searching with a hunted look for an avenue of escape from the reviver of memories too painful to be resurrected.

"I'll walk with you to the end of the drive," Catryn offered casually, displaying ten aubergine-tipped finger-nails as she cupped her hands around a cigarette. A brief skirt of the same colour hugged her slim thighs, and as she walked chubby-heeled sandals made poetry out of steel-slim ankles and long slender legs. "I mustn't stray far from the foyer because I'm on duty," she pouted her annoyance. "As this is my first week as resident courier I daren't take too many liberties until I find out how the land lies. Some hotels treat their couriers like dirt and others just the opposite – believe me, glamorous though my job might seem, it's darned hard work and were it not for the fact that I'm expecting it to lead me to a rich, handsome husband I'd have given it the chuck a long time ago."

"You would marry just for money?" Hazel gasped.

"Of course, dearie," Catryn laughed, "and so will you if ever you have the chance!" As wicked blue eyes swept over Hazel's pastel sunsuit and neat white sandals she murmured, "Not that that possibility is

29

ever likely to arise . . ."

"Hazel, *cara*, I was just about to seek you out! The little one is becoming impatient, and you did seem to be taking an extraordinarily long time." The end of Catryn's sentence was swallowed in a gasp of awe when Tio Garcia stepped from his limousine to take Hazel's arm. The parcel she was holding was immediately confiscated by the hovering chauffeur as Carmen's childish voice trebled from the depths of the car, "Hazel, we've missed you dreadfully, you've been gone hours!"

"Don't exaggerate, my pet," Hazel laughed, comforted by their concern. "I met a school friend who's come here to work in the hotel, and naturally we began talking. However, I won't keep you waiting any longer, I'm ready to go." Quickly, she extended a hand in Catryn's direction. "Goodbye, and I hope you find your work at the hotel enjoyable."

"Tut, tut!" Tio Garcia exclaimed, his eyes taking their fill of Catryn with the enthusiasm of a Spaniard half his age. "If, as you say, this young lady is a long-lost friend, then I insist you introduce us so that I might invite her to share our lunch!"

To refuse the old man's gallant invitation was the most vexing thing Catryn had ever been called upon to do. She struggled visibly with temptation, then, to Hazel's relief, declined. "I'm sorry, *señor*, I'm on duty until eight this evening. But I'm free all day tomorrow," she remembered hastily, "and I'd love to meet up with you then."

"Regrettably, we seldom visit this part of the island," he sighed. "We would not be here today were it not that the Marqués was too busy to accompany his wife,

so the Marquesa and I decided to bring the child on an outing.''

"Who," Catryn questioned blankly, "is the Marquesa? Not Hazel...?"

Tired of being ignored, Carmen breached the confused silence by jumping up and down on the seat and yelling, "*Si, si,* isn't it exciting! The wedding was held only a few days ago in the private chapel of the Casa de Drach! I was to be bridesmaid, but Tio..."

"That's enough, Carmen!" Hazel's unexpected sharpness brought the child to a sudden halt, but enough had been said to bring an inquisitive sparkle to Catryn's eyes. Hazel felt almost sick when, bringing into play her old trick of hiding acid beneath sweetness, Catryn appealed to the susceptible old *señor.*

"It's so delightful to learn that I have a friend on the island. Even if she is rather far away it's comforting to know that even in the midst of strangers I'm not alone." Hazel could have sworn there was a sob in her voice when she continued playing upon Tio Garcia's chivalry. "But perhaps I am being too presumptuous – if Hazel is now a Marquesa she might not want to be reminded of earlier days..."

Tio Garcia flung back his head and laughed. "Nonsense!" he denied, then, totally carried away, he issued the invitation for which Catryn was angling. "As you two girls must have lots to discuss, this is what I propose. We will leave you now, but at eight o'clock we will return and take you back with us to the Casa where you can stay the night and be brought back the following day in time to resume your duties. I know Francisco is worried that pressure of work forces him to leave Hazel

31

too much on her own, so he'll be delighted to receive an old friend whose presence will alleviate her loneliness. What do you think, Hazel, is that not a marvellous solution?"

Catryn's malicious smile dared Hazel to upset Tio Garcia's happiness, so she felt she had no choice but to force a smile on to lips too frozen to pretend and to nod agreement.

"*Bien*! It is agreed!" He bowed low over Catryn's hand. "*Adios, señorita,* until this evening."

"*Mil gracias, señor,*" she husked, masking satisfaction with grateful humility. "I shall count the hours!"

The excursion should have held delight, but Hazel had to strive to project enjoyment as they toured the resort's souvenir shops, sipped *limonada* at a table shaded by a gaily striped umbrella and wandered along the one main avenue which ran the full length of the beach where bodies sporting every shade of tan were being slowly basted under the rays of an increasingly hot sun. Carmen was fascinated by the pedalos, unsinkable tin boats that were propelled through the water by a pedal action similar to that of a bicycle but, judging from the squeals of their occupants, much more fun.

"May we try one, Hazel? Tio? Please ...!" she pleaded, dancing from one foot to the other in excited anticipation.

Tio Garcia looked doubtful. "I regret, such pastimes are beyond me, *niña*, but I have no objection to finding myself a quiet spot in the shade if Hazel wishes to indulge your whim."

Carmen held her breath for a painfully long interval

32

as expressions of doubt, uncertainty, then finally wavering chased across Hazel's face. "Well, we do have swimsuits, and if you're quite sure it's safe . . ."

"Quite safe," he assured her with a twinkle that mocked her timidity, "I have yet to hear of any harm arising from these small boats. Besides, you need not go far from the shore, the little one will be content to paddle along the water's edge where the crowd is thickest." There certainly was a reassuring number of swimmers splashing around in the shallows and the clear blue water held the promise of a breeze too tempting to deny.

"Very well," she relieved Carmen's anxiety, "let's go!" It took less than a minute to slip out of the dresses covering their swimsuits and five minutes later they were being helped into a brilliant red *pedalo* that rode the swell of water with confidence. At first, they could not co-ordinate their pedal action because Carmen's small feet persisted in slipping off the pedals, but when Hazel discovered she could control the boat easily by herself, Carmen knelt on the seat to watch the sparkling waterfall of spray churning out behind them. For a while they played about in the shallows, but as Hazel became more proficient the peace and quiet of deeper waters tempted her farther from shore.

"Look, Hazel, look! I see a shark!" Carmen was bent almost double over the side peering through water fathoms deep yet clear enough to render visible the contours of the sea bed. Hazel stopped paddling and relaxed, exploring the novelty of being rocked against the bosom of the sea. "Nonsense!" she mocked, "you know very well those dark patches are clumps of sea-

weed!" Carmen giggled, unrepentant, and continued with her fascinating imaginings while Hazel trailed her fingers in the water and drank in the scenery so beautiful it brought a lump to her throat.

Somewhere behind her in the crowded resort Tio Garcia would be enjoying a quiet drink, perhaps in one of the many modern hotels that sentinelled the front or maybe in a secluded back street café. To her right, rocks fell from a green headland to thrust a black finger deep into the sea, and to the front, calling upon a hundred variations of blue, sea and sky vied in beauty, then merged into one unforgettable landscape. The sun, lacking the vicious heat of high summer, bathed enough warmth upon the pert little boat to inflict drowsy content upon its occupants so that, unnoticed, it began floating towards the hazy horizon.

"Ahoy there, anyone aboard!" The very penetrating American accent shocked Hazel awake, just as a dripping blond head surfaced to peer over the side of the boat. "Well, well, a beautiful mermaid and a little pink shrimp afloat in a bucket!" he grinned into Hazel's outraged face. Carmen collapsed into a fit of giggles. "Which shall I choose?" he pandered shamelessly to her sense of the ridiculous, "the mermaid with the golden eyes or you, little pink shrimp, who ought to taste delicious!"

"Not me! Not me . . . !" she screamed with laughter as he dived under the boat to re-surface on the opposite side. White teeth snapped mock frustration as she ducked under Hazel's arm to avoid his reach, overexcited to the point of hysteria.

"Don't be silly, Carmen!" Hazel scolded, almost as

upset as the child by his abrupt appearance. "And please," she directed coldly to the unrepentant intruder, "will you exercise a little sense and allow the child to calm down?"

"I'm sorry," he immediately apologised, assuming such a fiercely straight face she felt her lips begin to twitch. But they were immediately controlled as she began lecturing severely, "You had no right to startle us in such a way, we might have capsized!"

"I wonder if you realize how far your little tin bucket has drifted during your snooze," he challenged softly, eyeing her flushed face with far more interest than she had ever before encountered from one of his sex. His look was so intent she was held by it, and it was with the greatest difficulty that she drew her eyes away to look around her. A gasp of sudden fear satisfied him that she realized his action was justified. The coast was far away, a mere blur on the horizon, and though there was no current, the buoyant tin vessel must have fairly bobbed across the water.

"Good heavens! How will we get back?"

He answered by pulling his lean body out of the water and levering himself into the boat. "Move over, shrimp!" he commanded, "captain's taking over!"

With adoring eyes Carmen did as she was bid. This blond god who had arisen out of the water was her ideal man – amusing, self-confident, handsome, and interested in small as well as big girls! Hazel was too relieved to protest; to have paddled across such a stretch alone would have taxed her to the utmost, and besides that her sunbathing had set off a headache which was rapidly becoming fierce. He insisted that he did not

need her help, so she drew up her feet away from the gyrating set of pedals and watched his bronze muscled legs thrusting the boat powerfully through the water. Once they reached sight of shore she felt ashamed of what now seemed unnecessary panic. The beach was still thronged with holidaymakers, swimmers still floated and cleaved the water, and when they deposited the boat the unconcerned attendant seemed in no way aware of their prolonged absence. Even Tio Garcia, whom she had imagined would be waiting anxiously, was absent, so there was no one but Carmen to add support to Hazel's gratitude when she took leave of the laughing stranger.

"Thank you so much for rescuing us, Mr . . .?" she offered primly, blushing awkwardly.

"Carstair . . . Robin to you!" She hesitated; it had been such a light-hearted incident, full of laughter and a gaiety previously unknown to her; now that it was over the price he demanded seemed so little to pay. "Then thank you again . . . Robin," she blushed again, painfully embarrassed even though she knew she was never likely to see him again.

"And I'm Carmen!" the child piped, then added preposterously, "and I'd like to kiss you, please, Robin!"

To her delight he reached down and plucked her from the ground. "And so you shall, shrimp!" he pledged, putting words into action. With cheeks aflame Hazel fled, dragging a reluctant Carmen behind her, but his laughter rang in her ears, telling her he had guessed she was afraid she might receive the same treatment.

They met Tio Garcia on the main avenue. He looked bored, very much out of place amongst the crowds of

sun-dazed tourists, but he smiled a broad welcome when he saw them approaching. "No need to ask if you enjoyed your excursion, *niña*, you look in danger of bursting with pleasure!" Guiltily, Hazel rushed in to forestall Carmen's obvious intention to outline in detail everything that had happened. Tio Garcia, she knew, would be shocked at her lack of discretion and would feel the fault was his for failing to carry out his duties with proper care. In spite of his age, he was sympathetic towards her English outlook, but Francisco would be outraged if he were ever to learn that she had been practically picked up by a complete stranger.

"Tio, I'm thirsty and so dreadfully sticky I simply must have a wash! Do you think we might visit one of the hotels?"

"*Ciertamente*! We have an hour to kill before we collect your charming friend, so if we indulge with you in your teatime ritual it should fill in the time nicely."

Catryn! Hazel had not forgotten her, but there were other problems much more pressing which she had to discuss with Tio Garcia; somehow she had to manage to get him alone! Her chance came unexpectedly. Once they entered the hotel Carmen became fractious, the excitement of the day and a missed siesta telling their own tale. A sympathetic manager quickly obliged Tio Garcia's request for a quiet room in which the child could sleep for an hour, and so Hazel and he were alone when tea was served. They drank in silence, he appreciative of surroundings in which he felt at ease, and she troubled, turning over in her mind different ways of phrasing the question that had to be asked. Finally, it came out abruptly, so lacking in frills that the old

hidalgo was startled.

"How did Francisco become responsible for the deaths of his brother and his wife?"

"*Ay dios mio*! What are you saying?"

"He told me himself," she persisted doggedly, "that he was responsible and that Carmen was allowed at the Casa only because her presence appeased his troubled conscience. I want to know why, Tio – and how!"

With an unsteady hand he replaced his cup, then answered as abruptly as he had been asked. "Francisco was appealed to for help and he refused, that much I know. What I do not know is how he can hold himself responsible for deaths that occurred more than two miles away from the Casa, in a fast car, driven by his brother who for years had been persistently warned about his reckless driving. As Francisco was in no way physically involved, I cannot understand how he can blame himself."

But it was understandable, Hazel reflected, piecing odd bits of information together until they formed a pattern. Francisco had fallen in love with the English girl who had passed him over in favour of his younger brother. A man of ordinary pride would have found it hard to forgive such a slight, but a man bedevilled by the temper of Drach would find forgiveness impossible. The young couple had pleaded in vain for help, then when they were half-crazed with worry the fatal error had been committed!

"Well?" Tio Garcia jogged. "Don't you agree that Francisco condemns himself too harshly?" She stared vacantly across the table, thinking of the tremendous burden of guilt Francisco had opted to bear. She

38

realized now that his words had been intended to shock, a subconscious attempt to purge his guilt in the whispered condemnation of the deliberately misinformed.

"Yes, Tio, I certainly do," she whispered, her heart heavy with sympathy. The nature of the beast was such he would scorn pity, rather he would stalk the path of loneliness, pretending indifference to pointing fingers while he courted solitude in which to lick his wounds.

CHAPTER IV

DINNER was served at ten each evening, and it was almost that when the car drew up in front of the Casa. Catryn was first to step out, and her head immediately elevated, following the line of lighted windows upwards until they petered out far above under archways fretted into rows of jagged teeth against the darkening sky. She made no comment, not even when Tio Garcia pointed out an inscription recording that the Casa had been built at the beginning of the sixteenth century by Enrique de Drach, the first Marqués, but her rapt attention to detail and her look of comical disbelief communicated plainly her amazed envy.

Carmen was still drowsy, so Hazel seized upon the task of seeing the child into bed as an excuse to escape being present when Francisco was confronted with his unexpected guest. Not that he would be impolite, good manners were too well inbred into his aristocratic bones, but she did not share the optimism that led Tio Garcia into believing that any friend of hers would be automatically welcomed. Francisco had ways of making known his displeasure without the use of words, and she foresaw herself becoming the recipient of rapier glances thrust through with annoyance. So she made her hasty excuses and ran in the wake of the chauffeur carrying Carmen upstairs, feeling in her cowardice absolutely no compunction about leaving all introductions and explanations to Tio Garcia's competent tongue.

Half an hour had gone by when finally she felt ready to join them downstairs. Carmen had gone uncomplainingly to bed and had been asleep in seconds, and the rest of the time had been taken up with a quick shower, a change of dress, and a light application of make-up. This time, she had chosen the green dress because after the hectic activity of the day its cotton coolness acted like a balm upon her flushed body, and it crisped around her ankles as she walked, adding vitality to movement basically lethargic. The sound of laughter arrested her progress downstairs, then a slightly open door spearing a finger of light across the shadowed hall beckoned her onward. A second burst of sound quickened her steps and she pushed open the door just in time to hear Catryn vivaciously holding forth to her attentive companions.

". . . of course we were proper little horrors, but there was no malice in our teasing, I assure you, we all adored her! Squirrel, Mouse, and Bunny were all experimented with, but nothing seemed to fit until we thought of Nut-brown, and that's what she's been to all her friends from that day to this."

An old, familiar pain reared up inside Hazel, the pain once felt by a slow-to-mature girl caught up in the midst of companions full of cocksure adolescence, too intolerant or too uncaring to feel sympathy for a friend whose only companion outside school hours was an old lady with a mind attuned to the ways of a previous century. Catryn's laughter twisted the knife in a wound that had lain dormant for years and revived memories of times spent pleading with her grandmother for nylons to replace white knee-socks, a pert beret

instead of the heavy felt regulation school hat . . . even her painstaking endeavour to shorten long, ungainly skirts had resulted in her having to endure a lengthy lecture on the sin of vanity as she was made to unpick every tiny stitch . . .

Tio Garcia was the first to notice her standing in the doorway, and the unguarded agony on her small pointed face sent him swiftly to meet her. With split-second intuition he wondered if Catryn really had been as friendly as she claimed with the girl who in looks and manner was her complete opposite. His hands pressed a warning around her frozen fingers as he greeted, "Ah, *mi princesa de los ojos de oro*!" It was a kindly effort, but in the presence of Catryn, stunningly turned out in a shimmering silver dress with bodice daringly cut, his "princess of the golden eyes" felt disconcertingly dowdy. Tio Garcia's smile projected silent encouragement as he led her forward.

"Darling!" Catryn scintillated, obviously delighted both with her surroundings and with her host. "We were just talking about you! Strange how little you seem to have told this handsome husband of yours – he knows next to nothing about your past!"

Surprisingly, it was Francisco who rescued her. She almost jerked away in fright when his arm reached out to encircle her waist, but his grip warned her to remain still, and to make doubly certain of obedience he cupped her chin in his hand and laughed softly in to her startled face. "I refuse to believe anyone with a name like *Nut-brown* could possibly have a Past!" he mocked. A tide of colour flowed into her cheeks when he used the hated name, but she made no further effort to

free herself from his embrace, although concious of his touch to a degree that left her gasping, she owed it to him not to betray their intimacy as play-acting performed solely for the benefit of their guest.

"I disagree," Catryn drawled, jealous of the inference of innocence. "We have a saying in my country: 'Still waters run deep' and you must admit, *señor,* that until now your wife has not moved in circles in which she would be likely to be tempted. So beware! Some day you might find yourself with a rebel on your hands!"

This amused him greatly, in fact everything about Catryn seemed either to amuse or intrigue him, and Hazel felt burning humiliation when with a shrug he released her to turn all his attention upon Catryn.

All during dinner she retained that interest, drawing forth not only conversation but also quick involuntary smiles from a mouth relaxed in humour. Hazel was relieved when Francisco left her alone with Tio Garcia while he and Catryn took a stroll in the gardens. "Hm, just as well some parts of the grounds are floodlit," Tio Garcia opined dryly, annoyed with his nephew and condemning himself for issuing the invitation he was now bitterly regretting. "I wouldn't trust that young woman with any man under sixteen or over sixty!"

"Tio!" Hazel was shocked. "You sound jealous . . ." She gurgled at the thought, amused by his chagrin, and he smiled back sheepishly.

"Perhaps I was rather smitten at first," he admitted, "silly old fool that I am! But no longer, *cara,* I assure you. Under that lovely icing lies more icing – the freezing kind. She lacks your warm sincerity and gentle heart."

43

Lashes swept down over eyes suddenly wet. Tio Garcia was being very gallant, but his flattery did nothing to bolster her confidence, especially now Catryn was here to spill her beauty into every corner of the Casa. Nervously, Hazel twisted the Ring of Chastity around her finger; it looked out of place on her small brown hand, the large flawless pearl dull as if sad to have been abandoned by its previous owners. Again tears threatened, but were not allowed to fall. Francisco had not sought any exceptional qualities in his bride, rather the reverse. Their marriage had been prompted by his guilt, by a desire to appease a troubled conscience, so what better bride could he have chosen than a spiritless nonentity whose presence hardly impinged upon his life, an undemanding mouse, to carry out with unquestioning obedience the job she had been chosen to do? The most important ingredient of their peculiar relationship was her insignificance; it ensured he would never suffer the distraction of having to cope with temptations arising from the close proximity of an attractive bride.

She heard Catryn's voice as she and Francisco approached the salon; it sounded high, its coaxing tone run through with a thread of excitement. "Please, Francisco, it would be such a feather in my cap! For years the tour operators have sought permission to take tourists around your factory – if I could be the one to obtain that concession it would mean certain advancement within my firm as well as a substantial rise in salary!"

At the shock of hearing his name falling so naturally from Catryn's lips Hazel stiffened. Automatically, she

sought his face when they entered the salon, expecting signs of displeasure, but his mouth was as indulgent as his words when he parried, "I won't have my workers disturbed by hordes of tourists."

"But they needn't be disturbed!" she assured him. "Our parties are always very well behaved and the outings would be carefully organized so that only those with a real interest in the pearl industry would be invited! Please, Fransisco, won't you at least promise to consider my proposal before condemning it out of hand?"

A surprising spear of jealousy caught Hazel unawares when he inclined his head. He was humouring Catryn in a way she would never have believed possible, a sure indication that in spite of his legendary distrust of English girls he was susceptible to the charms of some! Her feeling of rejection was not lost upon Tio Garcia, who determinedly projected her into the conversation. "Tomorrow, *cara,* if Francisco will permit, I will take you on a tour of the factory and showrooms. I promise you will find the trip interesting. You have heard of our products?"

"I'm afraid not," she stammered, aware that her answer would condemn her, but unable to lie.

"No?" Tio Garcia expelled a breath, and even Francisco's eyebrows rose.

"But I imagined everyone knew of the island's famous pearl industry," Catryn mocked. "Unless examined by an expert, the gems are indistinguishable from real pearls, and even experts have been known to disagree about which were the genuine and which the manufactured article!"

45

Remarks Hazel had heard passed referring to the family business became clearer, and the idea of a pearl-producing factory was so novel her interest was immediately aroused. Surprisingly it was Francisco who enlightened her further. Causing Catryn much displeasure, he deserted her to relax next to Hazel, then began lighting one of his favourite cheroots as he explained.

"Throughout every generation pearls have held a powerful fascination for the men of my family. The gem is incorporated into the family *escudo* and is woven into the very tapestry of our lives – hence the superb collection amassed by our womenfolk." He flashed Hazel a delightful smile, taking her so much by surprise that for one fleeting moment she felt at one with the cosseted brides. Blood was pounding so hard in her ears she had to concentrate hard to catch his following words.

"The first Marqués began the experiments. To him, the pearl's rarity was a challenge and the irresistible attraction it held for women made him determined to create a man-made pearl with a beauty equal to that of the most expensive gem, but at a price that would make it available to more than just a favoured few." He stopped to flick ash into a mother-of-pearl shell, unaware that his deeply modulated voice was hypnotizing at least two of his audience. Hazel leant forward, eager for him to continue, her huge expectant eyes claiming from him the smile of a story-teller who knows he holds his listener in the palm of his hand. "Trials were conducted over many years, but disappointment

after disappointment almost drove him to abandon the idea, because although some of the results were good, he would not be satisfied with less than perfection. He was an old man when finally his goal was reached and the resulting flawless, perfectly shaped pearl was the forerunner of many that were to give to the masses a pride of ownership and a source of pleasure known previously only to the very rich."

His lean fingers closed around Hazel's small hand, holding it up to catch the light spraying down from the crystal chandeliers. "Only one manufactured pearl is contained within the Drach collection, but it is the most highly treasured of all. Here, in the Ring of Chastity, is set that first perfect pearl, the flawless gem conceived out of hope and man's refusal to despair even against unbelievable odds."

Hazel drew in a startled breath; the thought that for weeks she had been carrying around on her finger the family's most treasured possession almost scared her to death. What if she had lost it? The ring fitted loosely, many times she had had to clench her hand to prevent it from falling off! She snatched back her hand and buried it deep in her lap. Never again would she feel competent to wear it, the responsibility for its safety must be shifted as quickly as possible on to shoulders broad enough to maintain such a burden. Francisco's nostrils flared, sensing a slight in the speed with which she had withdrawn from his touch. Hazel's lips parted on the verge of an explanation, but it remained unvoiced when he relaxed in his seat with a disinterested shrug and began blowing smoke rings to relieve the boredom that had suddenly clamped down upon his features.

47

Quickly Catryn seized the opportunity to renew her persuasion. Her silver gown seemed starred with tiny coloured sparkles when the light caught her movements and her hair was a smooth cap of gold framing the face of a slightly wicked-looking madonna as she appealed, "Will you at least consider my idea, Francisco?"

He raised his glass in a toast to eyes of vibrant blue, then drained it quickly before glancing obliquely in Hazel's direction and making his decision. "Very well, for the sake of my wife who holds your friendship so dear, I will allow your tourists access to my factory."

"Oh, thank you . . .!"

"For once only!" he cut in when Catryn jumped to her feet and ran towards him. She faltered. "Then, perhaps, he relented, "if the experiment is a success it may be repeated."

"It will be a success, I promise you!" she cried, looking ready to throw her arms around his neck as he stood up to face her. But something in his proud eyes, in the arrogantly tilted mouth that was barely smiling, must have cautioned her to be circumspect – for the time being at least.

The look of triumph she threw in Hazel's direction spoke volumes; she had been in the Casa only hours, yet long enough to sense that the Marqués and his bride were far from being on the terms one might expect of a couple newly married. Shamed colour scorched Hazel's body as she caught the look. Catryn was as as astute as ever, and as vicious. Years ago, as the pampered child of well-to-do parents, she had resented Hazel having even a crumb from her table. Friends of hers had been forbidden to associate with Hazel;

favourite teachers had been fed with tittle-tattle until subconsciously there had arisen a hardening of attitudes towards the girl Catryn had determined to make an outcast. It had puzzled Hazel then, as it did now, why anyone with so much should even bother to hate one so much less fortunate. A lump of dread rose in her throat as she, recognized the threat behind Catryn's triumph. Once more she was preparing to plunder! She told herself it did not matter if she lost what little regard Francisco offered, but to lose the love of Tio Garcia and Carmen would be altogether too much to bear.

She stood up so quickly that the glass she was holding overturned, spilling wine in a deep red stain down the front of her skirt. Her hand flew to her throat as, horrified, she watched it spread slowly, like poison into the mind, each ruined thread an omen of disaster yet to come. Francisco stepped towards her, but she backed away, the horror in her face so visible he drew in a sharp breath and remained still, his hand holding a proffered handkerchief dropping slowly to his side. A warning stabbed through her jangled nerves, clamouring to be heeded, a warning that she was playing straight into Catryn's hands, but the message came too late. With a strangled cry of despair she ran to seek the sanctuary of her room.

With shaking hands she tore off the dress which now symbolized the extent of Catryn's power, then she flung herself upon the bed to allow despairing sobs to rack her slim body. Her misery was so all-consuming that she failed to hear a tap upon her door, and a surprisingly concerned voice was her first intimation

that she was no longer alone.

"It was a pretty dress but not, I'm sure, irreplaceable," Francisco observed dryly.

Hazel twisted around, tears momentarily stemmed by shock, then blinked rapidly to dispel the veil of moisture through which he appeared alien and to her mind somewhat amused, bending across her bed. She scrambled up, not quite managing to suppress a last choking sob, and pulled the ivory bedcover over her bare young shoulders. His expression did not alter, but his obvious surprise that she should think such action necessary caused yet another revealing blush to betray her humiliation.

"As I have already said," he continued calmly, ignoring her discomfiture and directing a glance towards the discarded dress, "I did promise to extend your wardrobe, so the loss of one dress should not cause you such heartache. It shall be replaced as soon as possible."

Fury erupted when he disparaged the dress which, for all its cheapness, had been provided by someone dearly loved.

"As part of my salary, I suppose!" she flashed. "Conscience payment to appease any humiliation brought about by your attentions to other women!" She was utterly appalled when the words jerked from her lips, sounding like the accusation of a jealous wife, and trembling seized her when his nostrils dilated in a dragon's flare – the Drach temper was stirring! He stood erect, eyes flashing fire against features stamped with disdain, and though his lips barely moved his words penetrated her brain with stabs of fire.

"You are forgetting that your position in this household is purely that of an employee – a favoured, somewhat exceptional one, I admit, but nevertheless your status is and will always remain that of a servant!"

A blow would have hurt less; physical violence could never have inflicted the cruelty of a heart being squeezed lifeless. Hazel gasped at the pain of it, then, unbearably provoked, she dared to scoff, "That is something I am never likely to forget! But may I remind you, *señor*, that even servants have certain privileges, and I do not recall inviting you to share the privacy of my bedroom . . . !"

CHAPTER V

THE visit to the pearl factory was an unforgettable experience, marred only by an atmosphere – pleasing to Catryn, puzzling to Tio Garcia, unnoticed by Carmen – that hung in a cloud above their heads. Hazel, sheltered between Carmen and Tio Garcia, did not have to pretend an interest in the various stages of manufacture, but her rapt attention to detail helped to exclude many of the icy glints that told her she was far from being forgiven for offending the dignity of the Marqués.

Francisco drove into the small town that had sprung up around the factory to accommodate its workers, then parked in front of a modern, two-storey building very much at odds with the surrounding white-washed green-shuttered houses. Catryn hastened to his side, claiming his complete attention, leaving Tio Garcia to explain the various stages of production to his two companions. "First of all," he pointed out two engrossed young girls dressed in bright nylon overalls, "round glass beads are formed. See how the milky spheres are being dropped from hot rods of glass, and how perfectly they are matched in size? This unision of size and shape is dependent entirely upon the skill of the worker whose expert eye is her only guide."

"Please, may I try, Tio Garcia?" Hazel had to grab Carmen to restrain her enthusiasm, and she apologized to the girls for disturbing their concentration.

"We are honoured by your presence, *marquesa*," one girl answered shyly, her soft dark eyes following curiously the process of Carmen and Francisco, now well ahead. Hazel pinned on an answering smile, squirming inwardly at the thought of being the main subject of conversation around the dinner tables of the workers that evening: "*Pobre rosa Inglesa!*" they would be saying, "already she has lost the interest of her *grande consorte!*"

Her cheeks were still stinging when they passed on to where the polished glass beads were being coated several times with essences extracted from marine creatures plucked from the warm Mediterranean waters. After much dipping, powdering and polishing the jealously guarded secret processes resulted in tray upon tray of pearls, all perfectly reproducing the iridescence, beauty and perfection of the finest of natural gems. She was fascinated by the whole procedure and delighted also by the friendliness of the workers, so much so that she lagged behind many times attempting to exchange a few words of elementary Spanish.

"She has the *españolismo*, has she not, Francisco?" Tío Garcia grinned as she hastened to rejoin the waiting group.

"I too find Spanish people very easy to understand," Catryn clipped, flashing jealously, "but whereas I prefer the stimulas of educated minds Hazel is more at home with the masses." The opinion was expressed loudly enough for Hazel to hear, and happiness was wiped from her face, the sudden withdrawal leaving it pinched and bewildered.

For some reason Francisco became intensely annoyed.

"Shall we return to the Casa and leave the showrooms until another day?" he frowned, making his irritation plain.

"But I want to see the brooches, and the rings and necklaces, so that I can decide which to choose when I'm a grown-up lady!" Carmen wailed, stamping her small foot to emphasize her demands.

"I, too, am looking forward to seeing the finished article, Francisco," Catryn coaxed, confident of being indulged.

He flicked back his cuff to study the slim gold watch shackled to his brown wrist. "I'm sorry," he clipped, "I did not expect the visit to take so long and I have arranged to meet a business acquaintance at the Casa in one hour." Hazel felt his frown as an indictment levelled against her personally for causing the delay, so hastily she sided with him in an attempt to put things right.

"I wouldn't mind leaving now, I have the beginnings of a headache . . . perhaps, Tio, you could return with us another day?"

"Better than that!" he twinkled, mischief dancing in his eyes. "I will most certainly return with you whenever you wish, but as Catryn and the little one are so anxious to finish the tour, I suggest you go back to the Casa with Francisco while they remain here with me. The car can be sent to pick us up later and that way no one will be disappointed. Are you agreeable?" The silence that followed would have registered upon all but the most obtuse that the suggestion was unacceptable, but Tio Garcia's artless old eyes roved their faces with such lack of guile that no one felt able to object.

They came to the car to see them off, Carmen a little tearful at being parted for even an hour from her beloved friend, Tio Garcia struggled unsuccessfully to smother a grin of satisfaction, and Catryn visibly and unmistakably furious. Hazel shrank down in her seat, feeling somehow responsible for upsetting everyone's plans, but unable to pinpoint exactly where she had gone wrong. One thing was certain – far from extricating Francisco from an embarrassing situation his lowered brows and the grim contours of his mouth displayed amply his dissatisfaction with the arrangement. He swung the car out of the factory gates with the verve of a charioteer lusting to reach his goal. Chippings flew from under the wheels as without thought for the gleaming coachwork he sped along poorly surfaced roads hooting impatiently at any driver unfortunate enough to cross his path.

Hazel shrank back in her seat, wishing the copious upholstery would engulf her, thereby completely ridding him of the source of his annoyance. As a rule, when driving through the heart of the island, she enjoyed peeping into the dim interior of village homes through ever-open doorways, loved the spread of ancient olive trees with their suede-textured fruit and trunks curiously twisted to resemble gnarled fingers groping upwards into the branches, and the sight of glowing globules of citrus fruit hanging over garden walls was always freshly surprising. But today they were mere blurs of colour flashing past the window as he gave vent to the devil that drove him into mad outbursts of speed.

Gradually as his temper became spent, their progress

slowed. They were travelling along a coastal road, ascending steep hills with pine forests to their right and a dazzling vista of blue sea far below to the left. Hazel sat erect, craning her neck to observe as much as possible of the beauty that had beckoned her initially to the island. But travel posters could not do justice to reality, and around each twisted corner, every outcrop of rock, was scenery as disturbing as a sob. She did not notice the car had stopped until Francisco applied the handbrake with a sudden jerk. There were no signs of temper when he met her enquiring look, but puzzlement riddled his brow and more than a hint of resignation coloured the words that were wrung from him.

"I owe you an apology. I must beg you to excuse my unspeakable temper."

"I wasn't afraid," she assured him, misunderstanding completely. "I like speed, it gives me a glorious feeling of freedom – as if I were a bird, an eagle perhaps, roaming the heavens . . . !"

His eyebrows drew together, about to contradict, then when he suddenly smiled she really did feel like a bird – a small, captured fledgling with heart fluttering as rapidly as agitated wings. "No, not a bird," he corrected slowly, "an *ardilla*, a timid, dainty squirrel searching to establish itself upon alien ground – and I must suppose I am the monster who has brought to your great reproachful eyes a reflection of the fear felt by the gentle in the presence of the ruthless." It was said wryly, projecting an unspoken admission of the loneliness which so often plagues the aloof and the misunderstood. It wrung her heart, that infinitesimal glimpse into the forbidden territory of his mind, and propelled

56

the impulsive denial.

"I'm not afraid of you, Francisco," she assured him shyly, realizing the instant she spoke the truth of her words. She had been afraid many times, but only of the unyielding shell with which he was surrounded. Never again would she feel quite so vulnerable to his various acts of cruelty.

His profile lifted, etched with pride, as if aware that she had sensed a weakness, but when she continued to regard him steadily, refusing to capitulate, the first sign of melting coldness showed itself in a cleft running down his cheek which, when it appeared, left her breathlessly weak. "I believe you, *amada*," the cleft deepened into a smile. "Perhaps if ever again I feel the need to vent my temper upon you I will not be left feeling I have unjustly thrashed a child."

A spurt of laughter was released on a pent-up breath.

"Did I really make you feel that way?" she gurgled, lightheaded with happiness. "Poor Francisco!" Laughter died when he reached out to trace the soft curve of her cheek. His touch barely traced her skin, but left a scorching trail of havoc across her heart.

"You are a forgiving child," he mused. "Few women would overlook the insults I heaped upon you last night. It was for those insults that I was apologizing earlier — do you think that if I were to try again you would feel able to forgive completely?"

The surrounding intimacy was unbearable. Something deep inside her told it could not last, this magical moment of minds sympathetically attuned, the precious feeling that for once he was aware of her as a woman and not just as a child.

"What do you really want of me, Francisco?" she forced through a constricted throat. Then in a rush she clarified, "It's just that I don't wish to offend, to . . . to encroach further than you wish to allow. It would help if you could set a guideline so that my position may be made clear."

For once he seemed uncertain. A few minutes ago, she knew, he could have made plain immediately what her duties were to be, but an undefinable change had taken place, surprising to them both, and she sensed he was striving to be fair when he outlined slowly, "In the first instance my objective was solely to relieve myself of the burden Carmen had become. But now," he hesitated, tapping lean fingers thoughtfully upon the steering wheel, "now I realize how unfair such a position is to you." When he swept her face with an unfathomable look her pulses leapt, then subsided to a dull throb when he decided, "In future you must feel free to make any decisions you think justified so far as Carmen and the running of the household is concerned – I will instruct the servants that your orders are to be carried out without question . . . So far as you and I are concerned," he capitulated unwillingly, "the position will remain unchanged, except that whereas before you looked upon me as your employer I now feel we understand each other well enough to continue as friends."

Friends! Suddenly the word was hateful! Friendship with Francisco, Hazel imagined, would be a lukewarm, almost non-existent relationship barely one step advanced of the employer-employee status they had just abandoned. She was bewildered by the ache of disappointment throbbing through her words when

she accepted with forced brightness, "That's fine by me. Thank you for being so understanding."

As the journey continued she basked in the novelty of his amused indulgence and played the dangerous but delightful game of imagining life as it might be if ever his indulgence should grow into an emotion more lasting, more demanding.

Love! The word presented itself with the impact of ice upon her warm heart. She stared blankly out of the window, her hands tightly clenched, grappling with a storm of feeling that left her with nerve ends tingling and a heartbeat so erratic she felt faint. She faced a moment of truth, a time to acknowledge honestly the fact that had lain buried beneath the excuses and evasions that had convinced neither herself nor Tio Garcia when she had tried to explain her acceptance of Francisco's proposal. It had begun that morning on the beach, on their very first encounter, catching her so unprepared she had not been able to believe, much less cope. But now it had to be faced!

Gradually, as confusion subsided and her trembling body relaxed, her mouth lifted in the beginnings of a smile. An invisible burden of guilt had lifted from her heart, enabling it, for the first time in weeks, to beat freely and with renewed optimism. She felt relief and an unbelievable happiness as she recognized that the vows she had taken and the promises she had made had sprung not from lies but from the deep love felt for her bridegroom by an adoring bride . . .

When assisting her from the car in front of the Casa, Francisco was startled by a smile of sudden sweetness. Firmly she checked an impulse to communicate further,

and swept gold-tipped lashes over eyes alight with happiness. It was silly to expect him to share in the revelation, she scolded herself, causing him further puzzlement by adopting, with the swiftness of sun disappearing behind rainclouds, an attitude of cool indifference. "Your visitor has arrived, Francisco," she nodded, curious about the owner of the raffish red sports car parked further along the drive.

He barely spared it a glance before entering the Casa. "Our business won't take long," he assured her, his hand reaching towards the door behind which his guest waited. "I'll get rid of him as quickly as possible, then, if your headache is not too painful, perhaps you will join me for lunch?"

Hazel drew in a shaky breath: for once he was not *demanding!* "Yes, I'd like that," she stammered, ignoring his reference to the non-existent headache, "I'll just slip upstairs and change." As she showered and slipped into an orange sundress the memory of his inscrutable look remained with her. Perhaps, she mused, there was such a thing as thought transference and two minds really could converse silently. Wishful thinking? Perhaps. But her newly awakened love was so all-enveloping she would not have been surprised to see *I love him!* emblazoned across her face. She sped to the mirror, then sighed with relief. Nothing showed except cheeks pink with excitement, eyes glowing golden, and a pink mouth that however hard she tried would not discard its tremulous tilt of expectancy.

Francisco's guest was just taking his leave when she ran downstairs to the accompaniment of tinkling bells. The sounds encroached upon the men's conversation,

causing a momentary lull that was broken by the amazed ejaculation.

"Great Scott, *Hazel*! I've scoured the resort searching for you!"

"Robin! . . . Mr. Carstair . . . how nice to see you again!" she replied gaily, in love with all the world.

"You are acquainted with my wife, *señor*?" Francisco questioned coldly.

An explanation faltered on Hazel's lips, then died with a shiver as she became conscious of chill hanging like a smoke cloud about the gloomy hall.

"Your wife!" A soundless whistle escaped Robin's lips while at the same time he projected towards her a look of reproach which managed to suggest a degree of intimacy far removed from the reality of their informal encounter.

"Well," Francisco demanded, "have you or have you not been introduced?"

"We met on the beach yesterday," she tilted, angry with Robin and furiously resenting Francisco's haughty censure. When his eyebrows elevated, she forestalled his intention to speak. "Carmen and I spent a very enjoyable hour with Robin. We drifted out to sea in a *pedalo* and he very kindly came to our rescue. We introduced ourselves . . ." she petered out, hiding dismay behind a look of defiance.

She had to weather the icy glint that chilled across her before it came to rest upon Robin. "I am grateful to you, Señor Carstair, for extricating my wife from the result of her folly. Perhaps, in this instance, lack of propriety may be excused if we take into consideration your different nationality and your ignorance of our

ways. Please do not feel offended if I warn you against adopting such procedure as a habit. The women of my country are not used to being accosted by strangers and, were my wife not English by birth, she would have found such action most offensive."

The implication was obvious. Not only did it penetrate Robin's fairly thick skin that he was being delicately roasted, it was made plain that Hazel too lacked necessary refinement. She could have wilted there under Francisco's frown and under the scrutiny of his ancestors, their features immortalized by the strokes of a supercilious brush. No doubt now, his offer of friendship would be withdrawn, and with it the promised concessions that were a part of that friendship – a free hand with Carmen and *complete charge of the household*! She hardly recognized her own voice asking, "Why not stay with us for a couple of days, Robin? As my husband can spare very little time from his work, Carmen and I are often lonely. It would be fun to renew our short acquaintance."

Even Robin, for all his brash self-confidence, was taken aback by the suggestion. His glance sketched curiously over Francisco's taut profile, then lingered upon the bowed head of the girl visibly overwhelmed by her own temerity. As he hesitated, a roar filled the Casa, echoing along dark passageways, shuddering fragile ornaments upon their stands, and setting the staircase jangling with the noise of discordant bells. Every muscle in Hazel's body tensed at the sound and her wide eyes flew immediately to Francisco's face as if expecting to see anger flaming hot from snorting nostrils. Lightning flashed and Robin took a protective

step towards her, impelled by her look of terror. "Don't be scared, Hazel. If you really want me to I'll stay!" he shouted through a second clash of thunder. But she did not hear him, because with one last despairing look at Francisco she had clapped her hands over her ears and run to escape the presence of what she was convinced was the displeasure of the unreined monster.

CHAPTER VI

THE storm lasted all evening, thunderous sounds trembled the very foundations of the Casa, sword thrusts of lightning searched dark, mysterious corners, and wind tore through outside passageways sighing condemnation of the eruption into life of long-dormant strength. It would have been a relief to cry great tears of grief such as were being spattered, round as coins upon the windows and marble-floored patio. They might have marked the despair of all previous Drach brides, those sobbing raindrops, bemoaning the folly of a girl who when almost within earshot of a dragon's purr had opted instead for a provoked roar. Hazel flinched inwardly at each thrust of the elements, trying to look composed within the circle of guests chatting casually in the main *sala*, but conscious always of Francisco who, though pleasantly hospitable as always to his guests, conveyed to her by his very formality a threat of impending confrontation. From where, she wondered belatedly, had she found the effrontery to tilt at his authority? She, a mere employee, had actually dared to invite into his home a man against whose personality he had already clashed – and threatened to clash further.

"I must admit," Catryn lounged complacently against a brocaded settee blue as her eyes, "I feel grateful for this storm that's prolonged my visit. Not even the most stringent of employers could have insisted

upon my braving waterlogged roads to reach the hotel."

"But did you not know," Francisco's smile was inscrutable, "that I hold the elements completely under my control? A flick of the fingers," he demonstrated, "brings a lightning flash! A sweep of my hand for thunder," he laughed aloud when both thunder and lightning obeyed his commands, his sardonic amusement accelerated by Hazel's startled amazement. "And a hiss," he bent menacingly over her, purging his anger in eyes registering terrified disbelief, "brings the wind strong and wild to ravish all who resist my will!"

She jumped to her feet and screamed when a door burst open, projecting a cold breeze against her feverishly hot cheeks. "Stop it!" she choked, frightened to the point of hysteria, then crawled with embarrassment when everyone began to laugh and to applaud his realistic dramatics. Her foolishness was underlined by Catryn's: "Really, Nut-brown, you are naïve!" and even Tio Garcia, usually so sensitive to undercurrents, seemed greatly entertained. Only Robin was aware of her plunge into fear, and when buckling knees sent her groping for support he pulled her into the seat next to his and steadied her hands with his own. He directed a glance of utter dislike towards Francisco as he soothed:

"It's no crime to show feeling, sweetheart, rather a refreshing change, in fact, to discover someone without any of the hidden depths and pet neuroses that plague us lesser mortals." He seemed to intend a deliberate challenge when he raised his voice. "You are the epitome of my ideal woman – utterly feminine, totally visible, and pretty damned adorable!" He swept Francisco a glance of unsheathed steel and seemed

65

disappointed when after a silent clash which sliced through nerve, the Marqués decided to parry:

"I pity you, *señor*. Why do people never long for what is possible – always the impossible? However, do not despair, I'm sure that somewhere in the world there's a replica of the ideal you have sought and found – too late!" It was what Robin would have crudely termed a "brush-off", but expressed with such cool diplomacy that everyone sighed with relief. A nasty situation had been averted, but it was obvious to everyone present that the conflict so narrowly averted had merely been postponed until some future date.

The clearing of Tio Garcia's throat acted as a signal to relax. One could almost sense the subsiding of Francisco's wrath as he trod with panther grace towards Catryn, whose watchful body was rendered boneless by the warmth of his smile. Hazel drew a hand across a brow damp with sweat and felt terribly tired, as if she had been standing for a week. Vaguely, through whirling thoughts, she heard Tio Garcia enquire politely the nature of Robin's business and suffered a missed heartbeat when his answer indicated a semi-permanent stay on the island. "I work in the film industry, *señor*, a producer of sorts, interested mainly in documentaries. That's the reason I came to the island – the caves of Drach have a legendary beauty which I've been commissioned to transpose on to film."

"And Francisco has agreed?" Tio Garcia interrupted, startled.

Robin patted his breast pocket. "The contract is here, vetted and signed just a few hours ago by the Marqués himself."

"You surprise me," Tio Garcia admitted, sharing an unspoken belief that had Francisco not been a man of strict honour his signature would by now have been rendered worthless. No one was more aware of this than Robin, which fact, paradoxically, caused his resentment to increase.

"You have reached a position of responsibility very early in life," Tio Garcia appeased when Hazel made no effort to join in the conversation.

A grin split his honest face as he denigrated his talents. "Might just have something to do with the fact that my father is a major shareholder in the company!"

"I refuse to believe it!" Tio Garcia chuckled, his approval growing. "However, we shall find out in time. Many attempts have been made to capture the atmosphere of the caves, but although some beautiful images have resulted no one has yet managed to capture their intrinsic magic on celluloid."

Eagerly, Robin leant forward. "What makes the caves of Drach so special? I've heard the number of caves on this island estimated at some two hundred, so in what respect do your caves stand out from the rest?"

"The Cuevas del Drach are the most beautiful, the most spectacular, the most complete works of which nature is capable," Tio Garcia claimed proudly. "Formed by drops of water upon stone is a unique vault where everything lovely unites to form a secret world of enchantment."

Hazel felt a stirring of interest; she had gone as far as to join an expedition to the caves organized by the hotel, but at the last minute had withdrawn, too conscious of her solitary state to feel at home amongst

family parties and close-knit couples. Tio Garcia's vivid descriptions renewed her urge to see for herself the caverns of stalactites and stalagmites thrusting and reflecting in the deep blue waters of an underground lagoon.

"You are speaking of the Cuevas del Drach?" Francisco intervened, the flame of a match flaring above their heads as he ignited the cheroot jutting pencil black between white teeth. "Mallorca," he gave the island its native name, "according to the prophecy of one of our much-feared Spanish saints, is an empty shell. It is like a clay pot placed upside down, a pot which every time it nears a fire becomes more fragile and inflammable." When Hazel felt compelled to meet his look she sensed his following words were directed at her alone. "The day will come," he promised, "when by nearing the fire too often the pot will break and be devoured." Was he warning her not to pit her fragile strength against the heat of his temper? Her eyes dropped before the mockery in his. They thought he played a teasing game, these onlookers, but she knew he did nothing without a purpose, and fear singed along her nerves as quivering senses were subjected to a force so powerful it could have been generated by El Diablo himself!

She cut adrift from unbearable tension by jumping to her feet. "Please excuse me, I have to look in on Carmen . . . it's a ritual, she won't sleep until I've kissed her goodnight."

"Lucky Carmen!" Robin drawled, carefully avoiding Francisco's gimlet stare.

"Do you mind if I come too?" Catryn unfolded from

68

the settee, taking agreement for granted.

"No, of course not . . ." Hazel paused on the edge of flight, wondering what ulterior motive lay behind the request. It was unlike Catryn to desert the company of three attractive men for that of a woman and a child who up until now had shown very little interest in her company. She discovered her suspicions were well founded when, after ministering to the drowsy child, she tiptoed outside into the passageway where Catryn, who made no attempt to even enter the bedroom, had elected to wait.

"May I take a peep into your room?" she asked, already moving towards the ornate-handled door further along the passageway.

Too flustered to pretend politeness, Hazel faltered, "I'd rather you didn't just now . . ." but Catryn had opened the door and was stepping inside even as the refusal was voiced.

"God, what a set-up!" Her greedy eyes encompassed the pearl and ivory setting, trying to evaluate the priceless objects scattered indiscriminately around the bridal bower. Glazed with envy, her eyes roved, glancing once at the ornate bed, then quickly across to the door connecting with Francisco's room. The sight seemed to anger her, for she swung round to demand, diamond-bright: "What's behind all this, Nut-brown? Did you resort to blackmail, or was he pushed, because of a momentary weakness, into marrying you to protect your good name?"

The crude question flayed colour into Hazel's cheeks. No longer was there any pretence of friendship. Catryn's hatred could be felt, ugly and sinfully envious, snaking

between them. She recoiled from its sting, and sick to the heart answered with as much dignity as she was able, "Francisco would never allow himself to be forced; he proposed and I accepted because I love him and for no other reason."

"Oh, do me a favour!" Scornful disbelief registered in Catryn's every gesture as she paraded the room. "Little Miss Butter-wouldn't-melt, whose scandalized protest against my avowed intention to marry money almost made me feel guilty for the first time in my life!" With a harsh laugh, she spun round to torment, "I believe part of your arguments, Nut-brown! Obviously, he must have asked you to become his wife, and naturally a meek little fool such as yourself would be bound to fall in love with him. But there's got to be some other reason – and when I discover what it is you'll need to watch out, old friend. A full-blooded man needs a mate worthy of his intensity; he'll soon weary of your immaturity, and when he does I'll be waiting to provide the stimulation he's so obviously missing!"

When she swept out of the room, Hazel found she could not face the idea of returning downstairs to chat and behave as if the hateful scene had never happened. Catryn would carry on as usual, enjoying the cut and thrust of Francisco's conversation, accepting in an assured manner the admiration of men dazzled by her beauty if not by the brittleness some were acute enough to sense lay beneath the surface. She would not be missed, Hazel told herself as she prepared for bed. Tio might enquire about her absence and so might Robin, but Francisco would be content in the company of the

woman whose impact he had felt from their first meeting.

A cool shower did nothing to calm her. Still shocked by the verbal onslaught playing over and over on the sound-track of her mind, she pulled a listless brush through her hair, then let it drop motionless as she stared at her image reflecting pale through the gem-encrusted mirror. Her slim body, shadowed by a night-dress of ivory-coloured lace, barely made a smudge against the similarly shaded background. Her face portrayed innocence, except for the eyes which bore a woman's agony – an agony of hurt, despair and yearning to be loved.

She was turning back the bed covers when Francisco walked in. Without warning, suddenly he was there filling the room with his domineering presence. She stared at him, questioning as once before his invasion of privacy, but she heeded an inner warning to remain silent.

He advanced a few paces. "Did you really think I would allow you to desert your duties in such a casual fashion?"

"My duties are done," she quivered, distrusting the smile that was making mockery of his terse words.

She almost relaxed when he breathed softly, "So, as the little Carmen is asleep you reason that you are justified in retiring also?"

"Yes, why not?" she forced through chattering teeth. It was not cold, windows were closed against the chill of early spring, but her room had retained enough of the day's heat to make the lighting of a fire unnecessary. Until his entrance, she had felt no trace of cold.

"But what of your other duties?" he reminded her. "Additional authority brings greater responsibilities and you surely have not forgotten that mere hours ago you took upon yourself the role of mistress by inviting both friend and admirer to stay here at the Casa?"

"I didn't invite Catryn, Tio Garcia did," she flashed. "And I'm sorry about Robin. I know you don't like him, but I would never have acted as I did if only you hadn't jumped to all the wrong conclusions and practically accused me of being lacking in propriety!"

He turned her fire by beginning an assessment that started at the crown of her hair, highlighted auburn under the rays of an overhead chandelier and continuing slowly downwards, taking in suspiciously damp eyes, flushed cheeks and mobile mouth, then lingering deliberately upon the rise and fall of ivory lace betraying the agitation of a heart-hammering protest against new and disturbing emotions. "Whatever your reason," he stated coolly, "the fact remains that you undertook more than you knew when you opted to relieve me of my authority. You insisted upon taking a share of control, so I must insist you implement your wifely duties by coming downstairs to see to *our* guests!"

With a swish of angry skirts she swept out of reach, choking out the accusation, "When you've finished making fun of me, *señor*, I'd like you to leave."

The space she had created was breached in a couple of steps and two steely hands clamped her shoulders. The amusement she had taunted him with was totally absent when he swung her around to face him. "You will get dressed and present yourself downstairs in the *sala* in exactly five minutes. Otherwise," his menace was

unmistakable," "I shall myself assist you, and I've no doubt you'll find the experience less than pleasant!" He shook her, riled by her expression of hurt disbelief. The scolding of her left him feeling he had thrashed a child, he had admitted in a moment of weakness, and that was exactly how she felt – physically and emotionally thrashed ...!

Hazel fought to subdue a trembling bottom lip, biting deeply, welcoming the pain that blunted the edge of his verbal dagger, and the resulting tiny spurt of blood aggravated him further. His hands relaxed their bruising grip upon her shoulders but did not release completely. She was drawn forward, hypnotised by a glint like the swift unsheathing of a sword momentarily flaring in the darkness of his eyes.

"There is perhaps one more wifely duty I might call upon you to perform, little *ardilla*, if ever again you dare to disobey my wishes. The brides of Drach have all been pure, but you, *amada*, must claim the record for being the longest-reigning virgin bride. However, I warn you, if you wish to retain that small distinction do not goad me further!" She stiffened when his hands continued to make plainer than words his shocking intention, smoothing over curves, cruelly exploiting the grip of fear that rendered her paralysed, so forcing her to accept without murmur the utter humiliation of his touch. "You need not fear Catryn's more forceful personality, little squirrel," he murmured, his lips close to her ear. "Your restful qualities hold a surprising attraction for men who have suffered a surfeit of the polished vivacity which passes in some circles for charm. In fact, *mia cara*, in your own quiet way you can be

somewhat more than disturbing, and I would not be averse to discovering what thoughts and desires seethe under that cool little brow."

His voice deepened, as if surprised by his own words, then he pushed her away. A wave of lavender perfume was all that separated them when he grated, "Do you understand what is implied?" A great shuddering sigh was all the answer he needed. "Good!" he strode towards the door, leaving her to battle alone with rioting emotions, then lifting his wrist to check his watch, he repeated the warning, "Five minutes are all you are allowed. If by then you have not joined us downstairs I will interpret your absence as being both a challenge and an invitation . . ."

The door had barely closed before she began fumbling into her clothes. Buttons refused to stay put, zips would not respond to jerky fingers, but she battled on, seeing in her mind's eye the second hand of a clock inexorably sweeping away the precious minutes. He had left her no time for analysis, but twin emotions battled for supremacy, love and hate; desire and repugnance; fear and understanding, so that when finally she was dressed confusion was uppermost in her mind. She ran to the dressing table to flick a comb through tousled hair, but was distracted by her ghost-like image staring wide-eyed from the mirror. Had there been a grain of truth in his statement? Had she, unwittingly, managed to worm her way into his life so that, as a familiar object is valued only when admired by others, Robin's mild attempt to flirt had aroused possessive interest?

An approaching presence, heralded by the sound of tinkling bells as someone ascended the stairs, caused

her to throw down the comb in panic. She rushed to the door and stumbled into the passageway almost into the arms of Francisco, who was just about to enter. Her apprehensive, appealing look caught him off guard and dispersed the grimness from around his mouth as he smiled. "Such a pity!" he mocked, pretending disappointment. "I had begun to feel quite intrigued." Declining his proffered arm, she stalked past him with head held high, but inwardly she was writhing and fiercely resentful of a wave of longing so intense she dared not analyse too closely its roots of conception.

CHAPTER VII

DURING the weeks that eased spring gently into early summer life advanced at an unexpectedly tranquil pace. Catryn's busy season had begun and the army of tourists invading the island kept her too busy to visit the Casa. Not that Hazel ever thought of inviting her, but she often wondered if Catryn's few free hours coincided with the occasions when Francisco arrived home very late and uncharacteristically benign. Robin too was absent, finding his work at the caves so engrossing that he barely came up for air before plunging back into the depths of the earth to transpose on to film an atmosphere so unique that its capture had begun to represent not so much a task as an achievement.

Part of her job, Hazel had decided, was to breach the gulf of misunderstanding existing between Carmen and her uncle. She would have wished for nothing more than to spend her days in Carmen's company, delighting in the child's affection which was helping in no small way to disperse the feeling of insignificance that had plagued her all her life. But conscience nagged until, reluctantly, she decided some move would have to be made towards, if not friendship, then at least tolerance between the aloof *señor* and his small charge.

She nerved herself to approach him one morning as he was enjoying breakfast set out under a shaded patio. He looked relaxed, his casual cream shirt and tan slacks

76

implying freedom from ties of business. Her spirits lifted, perhaps her request was to be made at an opportune time! Soft slippers had deadened her footsteps, so she cleared her throat and waited on tenterhooks to be noticed. He was scanning a newspaper and seemed not to have heard her attempted intrusion, but just as she was about to try again he startled her by inviting lazily, "Stop hopping from one foot to the other like an uncertain sparrow and join me in a cup of coffee."

"I . . . I had some earlier, thank you," she stammered, wishing she could learn to control the flame of carnation firing her cheeks. She might just as well have accepted, she realized indignantly when, ignoring her refusal, he filled a cup and indicated the seat next to him; but this was no time to show resentment; she had a favour to ask which necessitated keeping the monster mellow. So primly she did as she was ordered, avoiding after one initial glance the impact of lazily assessing eyes and a mouth unsettling in its promise to be kind.

"I can hardly believe you have sought me out merely for the pleasure of my company?" he encouraged, laying down the paper to indicate that she had his complete attention. He watched with interest her struggle to remain composed. Since his threat she had avoided to an obsessional degree being left alone with him. Not that she thought his threat believable, but she had reasoned that the safest course to adopt was one of obscurity – how could he become angered with a flitting ghost who melted into the walls of the Casa whenever he happened to pass by? And as few words were exchanged between then, any risk arising from her unfortunate tendency to argue would be negligible.

She knew his patience was becoming stretched when he began tapping the edge of his plate with a knife. "I wanted to ask you . . ." she swallowed hard. "Carmen would like . . . I would like . . ."

"Yes? You would like . . ."

"You to come down to the beach with us!" she appealed in a rush. "I know you're very busy, but it needn't be today, any time that is convenient will do."

His eyebrows rose in two questioning peaks. "Strange," he answered coolly, "I have formed an impression that the women of my household prefer to see me retreat rather than advance – can it be that I am wrong?"

Carefully she pleated her skirt and sought a diplomatic answer. It was true that Carmen shot out of his path at every opportunity, but only because he had so often made plain his objection to her noisy high spirits. "Carmen can't swim, did you know?" she asked absently, her mind busily turning over future arguments. "I was wondering if you'd mind teaching her – there's no one else available, you see."

"Ah, so I am a last resort! You've explored every avenue before finally deciding upon me." The dryness of his answer might have indicated hurt in any other man. "I'm sorry," he gave an irritated shrug, "I have not the time. You'll have to teach her yourself."

Hazel's eyes rounded. "But I can't swim either!"

Was it so incredible, not to be able to swim? He was probably half raised in the warm Mediterranean waters, but that was no reason why he should look at her with such exasperation. He heaved a sigh, then stood up, holding out a hand to pull her to her feet.

Beside him she felt tiny and even a little precious when with a tug of a smile he capitulated. "Very well, little squirrel, if you also agree to be a pupil, I shall teach you both to swim."

Carmen was unenthusiastic. "I don't want Tio Francisco to join us, he'll spoil our fun – and besides," she stamped, her mouth pursing obstinately, "he doesn't even like me, so why should he bother to teach me to swim?"

Hazel called upon all her patience and tact. "Your uncle is a busy man, Carmen, so the fact that he has offered to spare you a little of his time proves he *is* fond of you. You must accept his offer gratefully, because by doing so *you* may be able to help *him*." The suggestion that her uncle should be in any need of help was an idea Carmen found intriguing – as Hazel had hoped.

"How can *I* help Tio?" she asked, round-eyed with amazement.

"Well," Hazel's tone suggested the sharing of a confidence, "you know how very late he works each night in his study, and how seldom he seems able to snatch even an hour's relaxation during the day?" Carmen nodded. "I thought," surreptitiously she crossed her fingers for luck, "we might play a little trick on him. By accepting his offer of instruction we can prevent him from overworking, but he will do this only if we pretend to be desperate for his help."

"You mean he'll think he's doing us a favour while all the time we will be helping him?" Carmen clapped her hands, ecstatic at the idea of outwitting her uncle. "Yes, let's do it, Hazel. Let's play a trick on Tio!"

Francisco was visibly surprised by the welcome he

received from his niece when half an hour later he joined them on the beach. Hazel averted her eyes, overcome by shyness, when his lithe, firmly muscled body, with tan contrasting superbly against black swimming briefs, appeared striding yards off the distance separating them. But Carmen had no inhibitions – an exciting new game was about to begin! With a squeal of pleasure she ran to meet him and was caught in surprised arms and swung high above his head. Hazel felt a thrill of sheer joy as she watched the laughing child wriggling in the arms of the man whose startled expression became softened with indulgence as he savoured for the first time the approval of his small charge. Above Carmen's head he searched for Hazel, directing towards her such a grimace of helplessness she forgot her shyness and went immediately to his aid. Carmen was laying on affection with a trowel, throwing herself into the skin of the part, but the danger of Francisco becoming suspicious had to be averted.

"Race you to the sea!" Hazel challenged, beginning to run, a flower-patterned bikini adding stem-slimness to her golden limbs.

"Quickly, quickly, Tio! We mustn't let her win, run, *run* . . . !"

It took him a split second to discard the cloak of aloofness with which he seemed always to be surrounded and the chase began. With Carmen still in his arms, exhorting him to greater speed, he followed with a swiftness of pace that brought him level in seconds. Excitement coursed wildly through Hazel's veins as his hard-muscled body flashed past her into the sea, then, impelled by uncontrollable impetus, she

followed, hitting the shallows with a splash that left her breathless. But when she surfaced her efforts were rewarded by the sight of Carmen, her arms tight around her uncle's neck, sobbing with delight, "We won, Tío, we won, and Hazel was ever so far in front!"

For a second his glance razed her blithe features before he observed dryly, "I'm not sure Hazel isn't enjoying a private victory of her own." But severity did not suit a face brown and sea-washed, with hair rioting in wet spirals above twinkling eyes, so he relented far enough to send her a smile, startling white against brown features, before heading out into deeper water carrying Carmen, half thrilled, half terrified, to begin her lesson.

Hazel found it astonishingly easy, when her turn came around, to forget her shyness and to accept as natural his light touch upon her bare shoulders and arms as he positioned her correctly before encouraging her to venture upon the stroke he had so patiently demonstrated. She was a complete novice, and nervous of encountering unfamiliar marine species she suspected might be lurking in the water, but when he scoffed at her fears to the extent of throwing back his head and laughing unrestrainedly she felt childish and even a little indignant.

"I saw some horrible objects once, pickled in alcohol and displayed in glass jars on the shelves of a pub in Gateshead. I was visiting a girl friend – her father was the licensee – and it was he who showed me the sea creatures he had collected from distant waters during his years in the Navy. They were revolting! Slimy and green – some even had tentacles!"

"I understand." When she surveyed him crossly he choked back a laugh and assumed an air of gravity. "Will you take my word you are in no danger of being stung by a king ray or grabbed by an octopus? We are still in shallow water, and not even a delectable titbit such as yourself will tempt denizens of the deep so near to shore." Her suspicious look banished the twinkle from his eyes, but nevertheless she felt it was still near the surface when he held out his arms and suggested, "Would you like to try again?" Every pebble and frond showed through the crystal pure water, even her toes were visible, peeping through sand refined as grained sugar, and the lazy swell of sea was a cushion of blue temptation, far different from the angrily racing waves she had so often watched battering the grey rocks and hissing madly over the shingled beaches of home. Tentatively she nodded. Carmen was building a sand castle on the beach, content, now that her own lesson had gone so well, to play within earshot and to shout occasional encouragement in a tone so condescending that Hazel knew she would have to do better or else suffer the interminable advice of one whose skill has been proved.

"Try floating," he suggested. "Lie on your back, completely relaxed, while I support your head with my hand. Ready?" It was heavenly; like a garland tossed to the waves, her body rose and fell with the movement of the sea, Francisco's hand a reassuring pillow, his voice murmuring encouragement as she lay contemplating a sky vacant of all but sun and puffs of cloud. "You're doing fine!" His voice seemed so far away her head swung immediately towards the

sound. He had deserted her! Her relaxation had become so complete that she had not noticed the withdrawal of his steadying hand and to her horror she saw he was now two arms' length away, swimming around in a lazy circle.

Panic screamed to her throat, as completely demoralized, she lost her head and began threshing the water. She felt herself being sucked under and opened her mouth to yell, only to choke on a rush of salt water. The deceptively somnolent ocean suddenly appeared as a greedy waste, teeming with strange shapes that were circling around waiting their chance to submerge her. She fought them with every ounce of strength, managing to rise above the waves long enough to scream before being plunged back into the hungry depths.

"Don't fight me! Calm down, you're perfectly safe, I have you!" She clung to Francisco with terrified desperation, hampering his efforts to tow her ashore by clamping a grip tight as a vice around his neck. When he went limp and they both began to sink she released her grip upon his throat, enabling him, in that split second, to duck out of her deadly embrace. He barely had time to gulp in air before she clutched out again, but before her desperate hand could fasten she felt a blow that sent her rocketing down into black, bottomless depths.

"*Chiquita*!" She wondered who he was addressing with such urgency. She wanted to open her eyes, but they felt heavy as sandbags, and as gritty. "Open your eyes, do you hear me? *Sacramento*! you must . . .!" Stupidly

Hazel pondered on the exclamation that forced its way through the sound of rushing waters to penetrate her brain. But a violent shaking intruded upon her slow thought processes, bringing pain and light, and an overwhelming nausea. "*Dio gracias*! Be sick, *niña*, as sick as ever you want to be!" And she was, humiliatingly so, with a violence that left her drained and too exhausted to protest when he swung her up in his arms and began treading a path upwards in the direction of the Casa.

Once there, servants were despatched with haste to run her bath, call a doctor, attend to an hysterical Carmen, and set out night attire for the sick Marquesa, who was to be bathed, then put to bed as quickly as possible. Even through her distress, she felt surprise at the terse, almost angry manner in which Francisco addressed his servants; his sharp commands ricocheted from walls and vaulted ceilings, sending up echoes to speed along the tardy who might just conceivably have missed interpreting his first demands. She tried a feeble protest, but was shushed to silence, then handed over to women whose eager hands ministered to her wants in the manner of handmaidens bidden to serve a queen. It went completely against her principles to allow such feudal servility, but the two women were so gentle and considerate, and independent effort really was so very much beyond her, that she murmured her gratitude and surrendered.

Later, when Francisco entered her bedroom, he was accompanied by a doctor, a slightly built, handsome Spaniard whose cool hands soothed as he made his examination. Standing by the window, his back to-

wards them, Francisco questioned tersely, "Well, doctor, how is she?"

Hazel blushed as she read in the doctor's smile understanding of the strain which he so often encountered from anxious husbands. "The rest of today in bed and a light diet – no solids and no excitement. Tomorrow she will be as fit as ever."

She jerked upright when Francisco objected, "What, no *medicina*? No special instructions? Forgive me, but I think perhaps another opinion . . ."

The doctor shrugged, but his smile held no offence. "Of course, if you wish it, but I assure you it is not necessary."

"It certainly isn't!" Hazel croaked indignantly, sending a plea for forgiveness to the doctor, who was snapping shut his case, preparing to depart. Her glance swivelled from the doctor and collided with Francisco's haughty stare. She shrank inwardly, wondering if the emotion he projected was genuine or just momentary dislike. His attitude was astonishing; never would she have believed herself capable of arousing within him such heated concern, but perhaps this was the way of Spanish aristocrats with their employees – to treat them on the one hand casually, almost as if they did not exist, then when trouble arose to elevate them to the status of family, making them then eligible to receive the bounty of the family's considerable resources. The Drach Family Health Service! Somehow a giggle escaped her, hiccoughing its way past unwary lips to emerge sounding slightly hysterical.

The doctor had just left and Francisco swung round as if to call him back, but he hesitated beside her bed,

brooding down at her small face, a delicate cameo glowing pale against a background of heaped pillows with not a grain of gold visible in shadowed eyes. When his hand reached out to trace lightly across her cheek she did not stir, but met his look, sensing a turmoil within that was preventing him from finding exactly the words he wished to speak. "I had to hit you, otherwise we both would have drowned."

Hazel lifted a hand to her cheek, exploring the swelling, understanding only then that part of her pain was physical and not completely emotional as she had thought.

"I'm glad you did," she smiled, eager to ease his remorse. "I owe you an apology – my foolish action placed us both in great danger." Her brow wrinkled as, quite involuntarily, she made aware her complete confidence in him. "I simply don't understand why I panicked – after all, I knew you were near." His tense jawline relaxed to make way for a smile. It was just as well he did not smile often, she thought; in repose his strongly etched features did strange things to her heart, but when he smiled his attraction was unbearable.

"Thank you," he said, but his warm look promised more; it promised a lifting of hostilities, deeper understanding, and as his eyes lingered, enjoying the confusion that brought pale cheeks to life and golden glints to escape from under downcast lashes there came between them a current of awareness – a cloud of potential dynamite that needed but a spark to set it alight.

The door burst open with a bang shattering to the nerves. Hazel sank back against her pillows, pallored by the shock of abruptly severed tension and feeling

86

unbearably deprived by Francisco's abrupt with-drawal from her side.

"Hazel, are you really feeling better? Did the doctor speak the truth . . . ?" Carmen flung herself on the bed, her impetuous Spanish strain uppermost, demanding to be reassured.

"Get down, *aprisa*! How dare you have so little consideration for one so ill?" Francisco glared at Car-men across the width of the bed, irate and impatient with the child whose relaxed upbringing was the cause of her so often behaving in a manner completely out of line with the standards expected of Spanish children. Her lips trembled as she looked to Hazel for guidance, the fun and companionship she had shared earlier with her uncle completely cancelled out by possessive jeal-ousy as the perceptive child reacted to the attitude of change in the air.

"Hazel is my special friend!" she challenged, tears tracing a course towards a fiercely jutting chin. Then, sounding the knell of Hazel's hopes in a childish treble, she attacked again. "It's your fault, all of it! We never wanted you to teach us to swim, we just pretended to want you to because Hazel suggested we should. We played a trick on you, Tio, but I don't want to play that game ever again if it means you'll be coming along to spoil our fun. I hate you, and so does Hazel! Tell him, Hazel, tell him . . . !"

But Hazel could tell him nothing – he had gone.

CHAPTER VIII

For days afterwards they did not go near the beach and a very subdued Carmen made no demur. Hazel had scolded her severely, once, for her impudence to her uncle, but then had withdrawn into a shell of silent hurt which indicated to the child some small measure of the damage she had caused. Their two wan figures flitted from room to room, Carmen a constant shadow following in Hazel's wake, anxious for an opportunity to atone, but frustratingly unable to penetrate the cloud of misery surrounding her friend. Eventually, her pathetic eagerness to oblige became known to Hazel, and the realization brought shame. Dear, impulsive Carmen was in no way to blame for the widening gulf between herself and Francisco; her own devious plan which had misfired, and Francisco's arrogant pride which had driven him into seclusion were the culprits that had engineered the void of misunderstanding neither excuses nor explanations would bridge.

It took great effort of will to pin on a smile and suggest brightly, "Let's go to the beach today, it's too warm indoors and there'll be a breeze nearer the sea." Carmen's expression of relief almost brought tears to Hazel's eyes, and the child's beam of pleasure, hastily subdued into a hesitant smile, made her vow never to reveal her newly born fear of the mass of blue water. A thrill of horror shot through her when quite unsuspectingly Carmen offered:

"Shall I get the swimsuits? It won't take me a minute."

"No!" Hazel recoiled from her own sharpness of tone, then took a grip upon her senses. "No, dear, we'll just laze today. Perhaps tomorrow..." she petered out, ashamed of her cowardice, but happily Carmen was too preoccupied to notice.

They had been settled on the beach no longer than half an hour when instinct warned her they were not alone. She looked up, shading her eyes, and had to choke back her heart that rose hammering to her throat when Francisco appeared, striding a path made golden by rays of sun. Like a majestic sun god he towered over her, casting a shadow across her face so that it appeared pinched and starved of vitality.

"You are recovered?" he asked, the politeness of his tone contrasting oddly against sharp, examining eyes.

"Yes, thank you," she quavered, digging her hands deep into the sand to hide their trembling.

"Good, then we can continue with your lessons." He dropped down beside her, his action smooth, performed with athletic ease. Hazel groped for her sunglasses, the only shield she knew he would allow, and felt only slightly less vulnerable when she countered from behind their shade, "I don't want any more lessons, thank you. I prefer not to swim."

He nodded, as if it was the answer he expected. "I came today for that very reason. If you do not enter the water now you will develop a fear that will haunt you all your life. I cannot allow that on my conscience, therefore I must insist you don your bathing suit so that we may continue your lessons immediately."

"I haven't brought one!" she flashed, nervously aware of the futility of opposing his indomitable will.

"Carmen!" He snapped his fingers and she came running. "Go to the Casa and fetch your swimsuits, *aprisa*!"

Hazel watched her small figure scurrying out of sight as if the crack of a whip was at her heels, then refused, tight-lipped, "I won't go in, you can't make me!" She almost felt the muscles of his will flexing, sensed his enjoyment of superior power, and wondered if the order he meant to enforce was his method of punishment. "Francisco, let me explain about the other day . . ."

"Don't bother," he crisped, rising to his feet so that sunlight camouflaged his features.

"It was for your sake – and Carmen's," she tried again, desperate to make him understand so that even if they could never again recapture the happiness of those moments the memory of them at least would not be scarred. But he moved out of earshot, concentrating his attention upon a sheet of sail far on the horizon.

"I'm here! I've got them!" Carmen hove into sight, already clad in her own prettily printed swimsuit, waving Hazel's scanty piece of green cotton above her head.

"Be as quick as you can," he indicated briefly. "I have very little time to spare."

Fear raced in hot and cold waves as Hazel fumbled her way into a one-piece suit, green-frilled, and light as her heart would never again be, before joining him at the water's edge with teeth chattering, eyes darkly enormous and a mouth a straight line of terror. She

sent one last appealing look into a face which knew pity only as a stranger, then when no compassion stirred she closed her eyes and allowed him to lead her into the water.

He came every day to the beach, coaching both her and Carmen until proficiency conquered fear and she was able to cleave fearlessly through the sea she was once convinced would become her shroud. But it would have been foolish to imagine any softening of attitude on his part; he came to fulfil a duty which was carried out with the efficient impartiality of a professional instructor. Only once did she make the mistake of trying to express gratitude, only to be cut by the snub, "Nominally, you are a part of my family – I hold myself responsible for your safety."

It was both a relief and a pain when he pronounced himself satisfied with their progress. Carmen and she had formed the habit of taking a picnic basket with them to the beach, but although Hazel hopefully packed enough for three he always refused to join them. Until the last day. He watched her pouring chilled soup made from garlic, tomatoes, onion, green pepper and cucumber from a thermos, then accepted with the comment, "Ah, *gazpacho*! You must have guessed my preference!" She had not guessed, she had asked in the kitchens, but he was not to know her smile hid satisfaction of her small deception. Crisp rolls with butter accompanied *jamón serrano* – sun-cured ham – then fresh strawberries pushed into peaks of ice cream ladled from a second wide-necked thermos, formed a meal that was to remain for ever a pleasant memory.

Afterwards, heat and contentment took their toll.

Carmen was first to drop off. Stretched out in the shade of a tree, her eyelashes drooped, then slid down to fan across childishly round cheeks. Hazel watched her smilingly, then turned away and blushed fiercely when she blundered into his quizzical gaze. "There is no sleep like the sleep of the innocent," he quoted softly. "Do you sleep so undisturbed in your *cama de matrimonia, niña*, or do you feel lost and cry out in the night for a companion to share your dreams?"

Her body flamed. Such perception was uncanny, how could he know of the many nights she had awakened in that great canopied bridal bed with his name drowned in salt tears upon her lips. *He could not know —* and must never guess! "I try not to dream, *señor*," she strove for flippancy. "Reality is so much more satisfying, I've found. Though dreams might make me a princess, beautiful as night, morning comes and daylight does not flatter."

Her chin was grasped in fingers suddenly rough. "But daylight can flatter, *niña*! Not the conventional beauty, perhaps, the kind that needs artifice to enhance, but the beauty of the flower who sleeps away the dark hours and awakes to the kiss of the sun."

Her pulses were hammering alarmingly; she could not bear his touch, yet could not bear to move away. "Are you likening me to a flower, *señor*?" the jest rasped her throat. "If so, which one of your exotic tropical species do I resemble?"

Her eyes were dark with hurt, doubly painful because it was self-inflicted. For long seconds he probed that hurt, unearthing every secret fear, dissecting her scared, lonely heart until he was satisfied that each

secret corner was bare. Then he sighed, releasing his grip upon the small pointed chin that lifted instinctively as if to weather a blow.

"I visited your country once," he recalled obliquely, "only to curse the chill of your English climate. But one particular day as I walked through the countryside I discovered a flower of enchantment. A daisy, I later learnt, a tight green bud on a slender stem, with petals of cool white tipped with rose, and in its centre a secret heart that showed golden only when sunwashed with happiness."

His eyes flicked over her slim body sheathed in green, then travelled to where colour tipped white cheeks to the flush of rose. He stood up quickly, pulling her to her feet beside him. To steady her, his arm looped her waist, then drew her forward until his warm breath stirred the spread of lashes fanning her cheeks. Taut silence stretched into infinity, it was as if the sea had ceased murmuring, birds had folded their wings and the earth paused in revolution, curiosity captured by the tableau.

"Golden heart," he murmured, "will you sleep more peacefully during the dark hours if I assure you that fulfilment will come with the dawn?"

Her mind teemed with confusion. She needed to think out his words alone, to savour them, and to sort out truth from attempted reassurance. To procrastinate, she ignored his question to ask one of her own. "And what of you, Francisco, do you rest soundly knowing you can manipulate all of us into whatever state of mind you wish?"

He laughed without humour, bitterly, with a visual

twist of his lips.

"Do I really need to answer that question, *niña*, when it is well known the wicked can never find rest?" When he released her and walked away the ocean resumed its sighing, the birds stirred, and the earth moved under her feet with a jolt that reached her heart, that cold, empty thing that had lived a lifetime of hope during the seconds the earth stood still.

Catryn arrived at the Casa that evening. Never one to hesitate to take advantage of a friendship, she had a favour to ask and she barely took time to greet them before launching her project. "Francisco, we have had many requests from tourists anxious to visit a local 'stately home', and I was wondering if you would consider throwing open the Casa for a couple of hours each week. We will ensure the minimum of inconvenience to yourself," she added hastily, "and of course great care will be taken to make sure nothing of value is touched by prying hands."

They were in the main *sala* sipping pre-dinner drinks. Tio Garcia had invited himself to dinner and Hazel had anticipated a pleasant evening; Francisco always strove to appear affable whenever his uncle made an appearance. But attention was centred upon Catryn the moment she arrived, flushed and apologetic, looking outstandingly lovely in a filmy outfit of a shade of blue that softened the hardness of her eyes and sighed around her ankles as she walked, giving to her an illusionary appearance of drifting within a soft blue cloud. Francisco's eyes kindled as he relaxed in his chair, twisting a goblet of wine between lean fingers.

With an indulgent smile he declined. "I'm sure you

must be aware that what you ask is impossible — nevertheless, I'm pleased you have come if only to give us the pleasure of your company while you accept a refusal."

Her mouth wavered, but she did not quite manage to return his smile. "Is that your final word?" she husked, projecting hurt far in excess of the importance of the request.

Tio Garcia fiddled impatiently with his glass, annoyed as always by the way Catryn monopolized Francisco's attention.

"Certainly it is," he snapped, reminding Hazel of an aggravated terrier. "The family of Drach does not parade its possessions for the entertainment of the public!"

Catryn sent him a look of dislike. He had become expendable, his usefulness had been proved as a means of introduction, but now, squeezed like a lemon, she was happy to discard him in favour of his nephew. Concentrating solely upon Francisco, she sighed. "I suppose you're right," her lovely shoulders drooped beneath a burden of worry. "I had an awful cheek to even suggest such a scheme. It's just that . . ." She hesitated when a tremble broke into her voice, then swept a finger across lashes sparkling with tears. "Excuse me." She jumped to her feet, poised to run rather than allow them to witness her distress.

Francisco was on his feet in an instant. "What's wrong, *mi cara*, what causes you such distress?"

Hazel was fascinated by the performance Catryn carried out to perfection. She watched her sway where she stood, saw his arm go around her waist to steady

her, and almost applauded the pathos of her words when she looked into his concerned face and murmured:

"I've been very foolish, Francisco, punishment is no more than I deserve." Her fingers raked through thick golden hair, disarranging its neatness so that she appeared innocently vulnerable. "I'm finding my job so very tiring, you see, demanding of me more energy than I possess. Perhaps I'm not yet acclimatized to the heat, or maybe I'm not as strong as I thought – anyway, last week I felt so dreadfully ill I simply had to take a few hours off work and when my boss found out he was extremely angry. He said that if I was not capable of doing my work I should leave, but I need my job, Francisco," she began to sob, "that's why I dared to ask you this favour! I thought if I could go to my boss with such a concession he'd be bound to offer me my job back and allow me to stay . . ."

"*Por dios!*" His chivalrous instincts were fully aroused. With a glint of arrogant displeasure that boded ill for Catryn's unfortunate employer, he snapped his fingers and decreed, "I will speak to this man who dares to treat you with such callousness. He shall be run off the island!"

"No, Francisco, you mustn't interfere, he has great influence – a word from him and I could find myself outlawed by every travel agency in the business! You must promise not to breathe a word of what I've said!" Catryn really did seem distraught; even Hazel's doubts were not proof against her show of distress. Realizing she had overplayed her hand and fearful of the grumbling of an enraged monster she suspected

might not be easily appeased, Catryn admitted with reluctant good sense, "My boss is not so harsh as perhaps I've implied – some of the fault may be mine for attempting to do a job which at times is beyond my capabilities."

"Poor child!" The realization that Tio Garcia had been completely hoodwinked hit Hazel like a blow. But, struggling to be fair, she had to admit that his defection was in some ways justified. The men of his race derived great satisfaction from cosseting their womenfolk even to the extent of accepting responsibilities of a relationship umpteen times removed. Catryn swung towards him, eager to enlist any ally sympathetic to her cause. "Is there no one in your family who will make himself responsible for your wellbeing?" Tio Garcia asked delicately.

"How I wish I could answer yes to that question, *señor*, unfortunately I can lay claim to no one," she husked, portraying heartbreak touching to all but Hazel, who had often envied Catryn the love of adoring parents whose spoiling had laid the foundations of selfishness in their only child. Her scandalized eyes mirrored her thoughts, and Catryn's hard glance dared her to reveal the deliberate lie.

"It is diabolical!" Francisco condemned, tight-lipped. "Young girls ought not to be allowed to roam the world unchaperoned!" His look was directed upon Hazel, her face shaded to solemnity by a weight of thoughts, and his voice hardened. "Especially not children barely out of the schoolroom whose knowledge of life is so scanty that one is compelled to introduce them gradually to harsh reality rather than allow them

to suffer at the hands of some less bound by convention or conscience!" Her head lifted, puzzled by his angry reference, but he had finished with her and was concentrating upon Catryn. He disliked being pressurized, and this fact was responsible for the reluctance with which he offered the suggestion, "Visitors to the Casa cannot be allowed, but in the grounds there are wine cellars where workers on the estate are allowed to hold their fiestas. If you think your tourists would be interested, we could arrange a weekly pageant — my workers will not object to dressing up in appropriate costumes to entertain, provided a small sum is offered as remuneration, and their wives will also be glad to arrange a barbecue meal which could be served outdoors far enough from the Casa to leave us comparatively undisturbed. If this idea should find favour with your employer, let me know and I will begin making the necessary arrangements."

"Find favour!" Catryn was speechless with delight. "Oh, Francisco, he'll be delighted and my job will be secure again, that's certain!"

"Good!" He smiled, then unbent enough to offer her his arm. "If that is so, then perhaps we can now go in to dinner?" As was to be expected, for the rest of the evening conversation revolved around the subject of the pageant and as there was much to discuss Hazel and Tio Garcia were each forced to adopt the role of listener, a situation which suited Hazel but which Tio Garcia found so tedious he made his excuses and left much earlier than he had intended. His exit caused so little disturbance Hazel felt she too was superfluous and she was just about to make her way noiselessly

upstairs when Francisco looked up in time to catch her creeping from the room. "Where are you going, *niña*?" he queried, halting her just as she was about to cross the threshold. *Child!* She wished he would not call her that, especially not in front of Catryn, who seemed to derive much scornful amusement from the description.

"It's late," she stammered, feeling caught out in some misdemeanour. "I didn't think you'd mind if I went to bed."

He flicked back his cuff and frowned at his watch. "So it is, I'm sorry to have kept you up so late, will you ring for a servant to fetch Catryn's coat while I get out the car to take her back to her hotel?"

"I'll fetch it myself," she offered hastily. "I dismissed the servants hours ago." She hurried out of sight of his raised eyebrows, vexed by his inconsiderate demands upon all who dwelt under his roof.

Catryn was alone in the room when she returned. She handed over the wrap without a word, but felt a tremor of trepidation when Catryn smiled. "You really must try harder to adapt to your new station, my dear," she smirked. "Servants are employed to work as many hours as might be deemed necessary. Francisco isn't used to doing his own fetching and carrying, and I shouldn't think he'll find himself able to approve such action in his wife." When Hazel coloured, but refused to be drawn, she remarked spitefully, "Rumour has it he was engaged to an English girl who threw him over in favour of his brother – did you know?"

"Yes, I knew," Hazel answered through stiff lips.

"He was supposedly demented at the time," Catryn watched shrewdly. "The way I heard it, Francisco

frightened her rather – he can be overpowering at times – and as the younger brother was his exact opposite in nature, she decided to throw in her lot with him, thinking she might as well have fun as well as money. Unfortunately it was not until after the wedding that she discovered Francisco held the strings of the money-bags and she'd let a fortune slip through her fingers." Strange, isn't it," she mocked, "that he should turn to you of all people for comfort? Or perhaps not," she amended unkindly. "He would be looking for someone completely different – men on the rebound always do – and from all accounts Carmen's mother was a raving beauty."

"Are you ready?" The smooth question caught Catryn off guard. It was impossible to tell whether or not Francisco had overhead; his expression was completely blank as he waited politely for Catryn. But when she swept past him to go to the car he hesitated before following, seemingly on the brink of words, then he changed his mind and after a piercing look turned away, leaving her free to release a flood of smarting tears.

CHAPTER IX

THE pageant was arranged to take place the following week. Catryn spent many hours with Francisco before the event – with the full approval of her boss, who had pronounced himself delighted with the idea – and her air of suppressed excitement was evidence that plans were shaping well. To launch the project, Francisco had agreed that they would all attend the first evening – even Carmen, to whom the prospect of staying up late was as enthralling as the event itself.

"We must dress up, Catryn says," she informed Hazel importantly. "The estate workers are to wear medieval costume and we at the Casa must set an example by appearing in the most colourful outfits we can find, so can we sort out our costumes now? Tio Francisco says there are lots of clothes stored in trunks in one of the unused bedrooms. Please, Hazel, say we can look through them and make our choice today?"

Having suffered previously from Carmen's dogged persistence, Hazel surrendered gracefully. "Very well, dear, you lead the way – I'm sure you've made it your business to discover exactly where the treasure is stored!" When Carmen scampered upstairs she followed thoughtfully after her. She had seen so little of Francisco the past week she had no idea what he might be expecting of her. Somehow she could not imagine his dignified personality accepting easily the frivolity of fancy dress, but then again Catryn seemed capable

of wheedling him around her little finger, so perhaps it might be as well to check before committing herself to anything drastic.

She hesitated at the foot of the stairs, the study door was partially open and the sound of rustling papers confirmed his presence behind the desk of hand-carved wood that dominated the room. Her hand lifted, preparatory to rapping for admittance against the panel, but before it could descend the door was jerked open by Francisco, who checked his hurried exit and halted on the threshold. He was carrying a sheaf of papers and seemed immersed in thought, but at the sight of Hazel his eyes sharpened to questioning points.

"Can you spare me a minute?" she forced out, hating the way her question had unconsciously reverted to a plea.

"I was just about to look for you," he admitted, giving rise to a panic-stricken examination of conscience as she strove to remember what wrong she might have done. "The catalogues I sent for have arrived. I'd like you to look through them and order whatever you need." When she looked blank, he jerked her memory. "The new clothes you were promised – I approached a fashion house in Madrid, one of the best, I'm assured – and they obliged by sending details of their stock. How unlike a woman to forget such a promise!" he jested, smiling so that a deep cleft of amusement ridged his cheek.

Fighting a sudden longing to run her fingers along its path, Hazel gathered her scattered wits and thanked him. "You are very generous, but really there's no need. All my belongings are new and you have have already

given me so much . . ." As lashes fanned down to hide her shyness she groped with nervous fingers for a non-existent ring on her other hand and a breath died in her throat when she felt his cool grasp.

"Where is the Ring of Chastity?" he questioned sharply, spreading out her unadorned fingers.

"I . . . I've put it in a safe place," she confessed, certain of being meted out penance. "It was a little slack, so when you mentioned how revered it is by your family I dared not wear it again. Besides," her sigh was full of tears. "I never felt it belonged with me; its long history of affinity with cherished brides ought not to be marred by its becoming the possession of an impostor."

She was prepared for anger, but his voice betrayed more savagery than wrath when he bit out, "So that is what you consider yourself to be – an impostor! Small wonder those around you attach so little importance to the fact that you are my wife when you yourself are so reluctant to face that reality."

His words probed the wound left by Catryn's derogatory remarks, setting her smarting. "A woman doesn't automatically become a wife by the bestowal of a ring and the exchanging of vows!" she retorted harshly. "Robin suspects, just as Catryn must, that our marriage is a sham. Marriage means love, and love is movement . . . things have to keep happening . . ." She faltered, aching to express her feelings but so frustrated by shyness she resorted to taunts. "You are afraid of love, Francisco, afraid of its meaning, unable to relinquish even a small share of yourself to another, which is what love demands! For too long you've been an island, a man apart, cutting yourself off from gossip and from the

unkind remarks of your neighbours so that now it's become second nature to think only of yourself – *your* wishes, *your* feelings! How can you deny me the comfort of pretence when facing reality means accepting the fact that I married an unfeeling autocrat!"

He could not have been more taken aback if an infant had suddenly exposed claws. During the span of silence that followed her accusation she wanted to flee, but was prevented by a weight of fear that paralysed all movement. Fascinated, she watched a pulse hammering against a jawline taut with disdain, then flinched from the impact of a look, riveting as sunlight glancing from steel, that surprised his dark eyes from their state of disinterest into alert arrogance. Centuries of pride carried in the words ejected through lips drawn thin with anger. "Santa Maria, is nothing sacred? How dare you allow our private lives to become a matter of discussion between you and your friends!"

Appalled by the realization that only one part of her impassioned outburst had registered, she pleaded:

"But you don't understand! I didn't . . ." She ached to disabuse him of the idea that she was capable of such treachery, but it became immediately evident that she was pitting her strength against barriers too rigid to give way, so she abandoned hope and with a last gasp of despair she fled.

The wine cellars were situated in a tower built some distance from the Casa on land which had in the past received little attention. Once, someone had attempted to cultivate a garden around the crumbling edifice that poked upwards into the sky a stone finger of contempt raised against those responsible for its rejection, and

small coloured lights strung between trees lent an illusory beauty to the roses struggling out of bud on the few bushes left unstrangled by weeds. But the estate workers had been busy. Trestles covered in snow-white tablecloths held rows of wine glasses waiting to be filled from large brown jugs containing sherry of every shade ranging from pale liquid gold to full-bodied earthy brown. Dishes of salted almonds and potato crisps waited with crisp cheese straws to tempt nibblers, and in the background, preparing for the arrival of the tourists, musicians tuned their instruments, experimentally strumming an odd chord or two that rippled out of the darkness, sending a promise of almost tropical excitement.

The party from the Casa decided to wait in the garden for the coaches to arrive before entering the cellars. It was a pleasantly warm night and they were curious to see for themselves the first reactions of their visitors. Robin, who had been enticed from his work by the promise of material for a future documentary, was first to notice approaching headlights. "Prepare for the invasion, folks," he murmured, then in a wicked aside he teased Hazel, "I hope they don't forget protocol when in the presence of royalty!"

She glanced towards Francisco, then hastily away. His air of breeding was indeed accentuated by the clothes he wore with such assurance that he could have stepped from the framed portrait of one of his ancestors, a conquistador of long ago. A velvet jacket the colour of dark wine added interest to his fine features, lace cuffs contrasting starkly against costly rings flashing emerald and ruby from fingers hovering lightly over the

hilt of a silver-sheathed sword caressing the calf of a lean, black-trousered leg. He seemed a true son of Spain, an adventurer so untrammelled he knew not the discipline of relinquishing whatever he might covet, a plunderer whose look was unsettling in its threat that whatever he wanted – he took!

Hazel had avoided that look since its first conception earlier that evening. He had stepped into her bedroom when, in answer to his knock, she had bidden him enter. At first encounter all breath had left her, then as she had waited his approval of her dress of heavy brocade, exquisitely embroidered with silks pink as a flamingo's wing, and a matching mantilla that crowned her small head with unexpected dignity, the spark had been born and with it a response from her so primitive she had felt wanton. She shied from the memory of his words, uttered coolly, but with undercurrents of warning.

"Tonight, you look as a bride should look, *amada*, untouched, innocent, and so very unaware. It was most remiss of me to overlook that such lack of awareness is proof to all who seek it that – as you so rightly asserted – no progress has been made. However," he had made no move nearer but she had felt stifled by threat when he had menaced in a tone silken terse, "fortunately that situation can be easily remedied. Soon, Marquesa, the whole island will look at you and think: Ah, there goes a wife who is truly *bienquista*!"

Well-beloved! To have dwelt upon his meaning would have been to court disaster, so she thrust it from her mind and tried to concentrate her attention upon Robin, whose candid, modern outlook was a balm to

106

her fevered brain. But even that was denied her when she was bidden to Francisco's side as the tourists began filing out of the coaches. English, French and German voices mingled in excited anticipation as the band of Spanish troubadors struck the first chords of welcoming music from their beribboned guitars and began strolling through the throng who were being served glasses of wine by smiling young girls dressed in flounced skirts protected by minute aprons, and blouses with wide sleeves caught in bands around the wrists, their neck-lines slashed wide to leave smooth-skinned shoulders bare. A huge moon playing hide and seek amongst the clouds lent an air of enchantment to the gardens, scattering moon magic over neglected bushes and softening the harsh walls of the tower with a sheen of silver so that the anticipatory visitors felt surrounded by romance – fairytale romance – within a setting of deeply-shadowed grounds, a majestic tower, and medi-eval atmosphere that called out for a hero and heroine and found them in the handsome Marqués and his delightfully shy bride.

To Hazel, it was as if she was forced unexpectedly into acting out a major role in a play; her every move-ment and gesture was noted by hundreds of watchful eyes focused exclusively upon herself and Francisco who, it seemed, had been cast as Adonis to her Venus. Adonis – the hunter who had disdained love – the simile was unconsciously apt; like Adonis, Francisco loved to hunt – human prey – but love he laughed to scorn!

His reaction to the notice they were receiving was surprising. He began playing up, showering her with

attentions which he bestowed with an outward show of affection much appreciated by their audience. His brown cheeks were cleft with laughter lines when he forced her to acknowledge his presence. "We are the stars of the pageant, it seems, so I suggest we forget our differences and pretend an enjoyment of each other's company for tonight, at least. Who knows," his teeth snapped, "you might discover after a while that I am not so far removed from being human as you think."

There was no doubt in her mind that he was human, his warm breath upon her brow, the energy emitting from his lean body, together with the captivating, reckless air he had donned with his outfit of plundering conquistador were all hammering out a warning against the folly of lowered defences. But some moon magic must have rubbed off on her too, because discarding caution like a cloak, she peeped a grave smile from behind the lace mantilla framing her face with the innocence of a coif and satisfied him with the answer: "Obviously, you're in a mood for enjoyment – I only hope I haven't forgotten how to play!"

Under his benevolent charge she blossomed, a moon flower living out her short span without thought for the limbo of tomorrow, and the claims of Carmen, Robin and Catryn faded as Francisco demanded and received her complete absorption. They passed through a wooden door set deep into the grey stone of the tower to enter wine cellars where more trestles and benches awaited occupation. As befitted their position, Francisco and Hazel presided over the main table which had an unobscured view of the floor space set aside as a stage for the evening's entertainers. Around rough-

cast walls were ranged hundreds of barrels, already tapped, each labelled with information about the type and origin of the stored wine, from which waitresses began filling jugs which were then offered along the lines of tables so that guests might decide upon the vintage best suited to their palate. When a young waitress hurried to serve them, Francisco allowed her to fill his own glass with pale liquid, then covered Hazel's with his hand and refused. "No, not *fina* – the Marquesa does not favour the dry nor the acid. Fetch an *oloroso*; it is rather heavy, but its sweetness will be more to her taste."

She knew nothing about wine, but found the tasting enjoyable, although the warm sensation she experienced as she sipped experimentally owed its origin less to pleasantness of taste than to the novelty of basking in his attention.

"Tell me how you know which wine to choose," she asked, watching a large German holding the contents of his glass up to the light, then discarding it without so much as a sip in favour of another.

"It is a matter of personal taste, initially," he obliged, bending closer to her ear as a blast of music heralded the arrival on stage of a flamenco dancer. "A novice rarely enjoys the pale, very dry *fino*, but as a drinker matures his palate almost always progresses towards the slightly acid in preference to the heavily sweet. But it is only by experiment and by experience that one can separate at sight the potent *riojas* of Castile from the lighter, rougher *valdepeñas* of the plains of La Mancha, or to tell the moderately dry wines of Alicante from the sweet and heavy products oi Catalonia."

Enormous happiness built up inside of her as the entertainment progressed and the flushed, broadly-smiling tourists abandoned their inhibitions to relish to full capacity the rhythmic tapping of the flamenco; the switch to pathos by a young girl who, sad-eyed and mournful, sang of the loss of her lover followed, with a rapid see-sawing of emotions, by the cheerful band of musicians exhorting everyone to follow them outside where a dance-floor was laid out under a canopy of stars and an enticing smell beckoned the hungry to partake of grilled meats and succulent poultry sizzling over charcoal fires, or to quench their thirst from a wider selection of drinks displayed behind an adjacent bar.

"Are you hungry?" he murmured, pulling her close as they swayed to the romantic music of throbbing guitars.

"No," she sighed, snuggling closer, happy to encourage the prevalent impression of an adoring and adored wife. When his hand touched her cheek she turned her face inward to meet it.

"Funny child," he smiled tightly, "you react so blindly to the least hint of kindness that I become afraid for you."

"Why afraid . . . ?" she queried contentedly, feeling his hands fastening a steel caress upon her waist. She was shaken impatiently, then placated with a half kiss that feathered across her eyelids before fading somewhere behind her ear.

"Because not everyone believes in naïveté, more often lack of guile is mistaken for encouragement," he said meaningfully.

"But you are my husband!" she teased, lightheaded with happiness and the small amount of wine she had drunk. "Why should you fear for me, Francisco? I'm not afraid, I trust you completely!"

"Are you sure?" he whispered, skimming her cheek with lips that left a trail of scorching heat. "If so, there is no reason why you should hesitate to come back with me to the Casa, *cara*."

Hazel stumbled and his grasp tightened. It was true that deep down she trusted him implicitly, but the *real* Francisco, the one she knew and loved, not this renegade whose look jeered, daring her to retract her impulsive statement.

"Very well," she conceded, tilting her chin in brave defiance of the threat that had echoed at the back of her mind all evening. *Bienquista*! he had promised; perhaps now was as good a time as any to discover whether his conception of the treatment deserving by one well-beloved tallied in any way with her own.

The Casa was silent, all the servants had been given permission to attend the pageant, so only the painted, superior eyes of bygone ancestors watched their entry into the hall. Francisco halted at the foot of the stairs and held out a hand to assist her. Hazel felt sudden foreboding when his lips quirked, betraying enjoyment of some private joke, and as her eyes moved swiftly from him to the line of family portraits it seemed to her agitated imagination that they were all smiling – the unkind, malicious smiles of those about to witness the downfall of one who has transgressed. A metallic clatter as Francisco discarded his sword caused her to swing round with a gasp, and she experienced a wave of bitter

self-recrimination when with an action full of meaning he discarded his richly coloured jacket and began casually to loosen the buttons of his shirt, leaving his chest bare so that flexing muscles were allowed freedom to stretch. His eyes narrowed lazily as colour slowly ebbed from her cheeks, but there was no mercy in his tone when he stated, "We needn't linger here, we'll be much more comfortable upstairs . . ."

Her leaden limbs did not respond to what was virtually a command, but when he took an impatient step nearer she found breath to appeal, "Let's go into the kitchen and forage, I'm hungry . . ." She tried to put distance between them, but he would not be thwarted. Two strides brought him to her side and she was lifted against his hard chest and carried forcibly upstairs to her room. The bang when he kicked shut the door echoed through the house like a shout of laughter hollow enough to bring beads of cold sweat to her brow.

She was beyond protest when he laid her on the bed; protest in any case would have been useless against a man determined to avenge outraged pride. With the cool reasoning of a detached onlooker, one part of her brain analysed his actions, remembering his angry condemnation of her supposed disclosures about their marriage to Robin and Catryn and his threat of retribution. "*Dear heaven,*" she cried silently, "*how he must hate me!*"

He bent over her, studying his reflection in pools of unshed tears.

"Don't look so reproachful, *cara,* by and by we must all learn the taste of tears." The mantilla was filched

from her hair, and her head laid gently back against the pillows. Shoes were slipped from her feet, then the necklace of pearls with its crucifix of agony was removed from its resting place against her breast. Only when his fingers began undoing tiny buttons on her sleeves did she appeal, "Why are you so angry with me, Francisco?"

One diabolical eyebrow lifted. "I am not angry, *amada*, far from it – no man about to make love to his bride has room in his heart for anger."

"You have no heart!" she challenged in a frightened whisper, meeting a look that drained from her every vestige of courage and hope. Dark passion held him in sway; a river dammed, or a damped-down furnace, would have no more tempestuous release! Like a bird tangled in a net she was held helpless waiting for the avenger to swoop and when his dark head lowered she closed her eyes and heard from far off his whispered invitation. "Your mouth of wild innocence urges answers to questions it dares not ask, *amada*. Come, share with me a thousand honeyed secrets."

A last desperate appeal was forced from her. "I want no share in hatred and scorn! Please, Francisco, please wait . . ." The plea was murdered, strangled by a kiss that closed upon half-parted lips to plunder and punish and revenge. As the coldness around her heart became seared with the heat of passion she held on tightly to sanity and refused to respond to the call of wild blood racing full flood and caresses increasingly urgent in demand. Lips that were merely submitting to punishment grew cold under his warmth, angering his emotions so that his grip tightened and pain mingled with

desire and became one.

Just when her resistance had almost reached breaking point, she felt a shudder ripple through his powerful shoulders, then heard an expletive that rasped his throat as he thrust her savagely away. Against the pillows her hair tumbled bright, contrasting deeply against eyes dark with bewildered accusation. He moved away as if finding the look unbearable and strode to the doorway where he turned to vent his frustrated anger. She shuddered from his contemptuous scorn, then something inside her shrivelled and died under the lash of his condemnation.

"Thirst cannot be quenched by the cold wine of chastity," he indicted savagely. "Be thankful I put from myself a childish thing."

CHAPTER X

Robin stayed all night at the Casa. The hotel where he was staying to be within easy distance of the caves was on the other side of the island, so he had accepted gratefully their offer of hospitality. Catryn was also present at breakfast next morning, having received permission from her affable boss to stay behind and supervise the clearing up operations found to be necessary after the wonderfully successful evening. Carmen was first to notice Hazel hesitating on the threshold of the breakfast salon. Sun was streaking through half-closed shutters on to Francisco's head bent in close attendance upon Catryn, who sat next to him – a golden girl, with sunlight forming a molten halo around her hair and lending added sparkle to eyes already aglow as she engaged him in animated conversation.

"Hazel! Are you feeling better?" Carmen scrambled from her seat and ran to meet her. "Tio Francisco said you left early last night because you were indisposed!"

Hazel felt her cheeks beginning slowly to burn and in her confusion sought help from the one person whose company she had hoped to avoid. His bland indifference as he responded to her silent pleas contrasted shockingly with the ardour he had displayed only a few short hours ago and, with the imprint of his caresses still branding her body, she shivered.

"As I've explained at least a dozen times, Hazel was tired and I decided she should retire early," he chided

Carmen icily. "Kindly be seated and allow her to eat breakfast without further fuss!" Casting him a look of sulky dislike, Carmen obeyed, and Hazel slid into a chair, hoping the battery of raking eyes were reading no more than confusion in her hot, embarrassed face.

Robin continued eating until he felt she was relaxed enough to converse, then giving her time to eat a roll and to drink half a cup of coffee, he demanded in an undertone, "What's the real story behind your abrupt disappearance last night – or," his look switched to Francisco's urbane features, "shouldn't I ask?"

Her knife fell from nerveless fingers, shattering discord into the peaceful atmosphere. Hastily she retrieved it, sensing Francisco's raised eyebrows and Catryn's satisfied smile. "It happened just as Francisco said." She choked on a particle of roll lodged in her throat.

Robin eyed her curiously. "You look different – I don't know how exactly, but there's a hint of something too elusive to name in your eyes and your mouth has a Mona Lisa quality that's driving me mad with curiosity."

Her nerves contracted. Were her ravaged feelings displayed for all to see? Had the painful emotional surgery she had suffered contrived to bring about what no amount of wishing could do? She knew she had changed, but was not sure fully to what extent; last night a simplehearted, uncomplicated girl had wandered into a dragon's lair and emerged a woman – less simple, more knowledgeable, and struggling to cope with a newly created shell of bitterness. Confused emotions were warring for supremacy; even while

trying to clinically assess her position unexpected waves of longing were surprising her young body.

Her emotions had undergone a drastic change. Francisco had tried to demonstrate dominance over her body and will, but her refusal to submit had aroused a monster that had turned to rend clawmarks of agony upon her heart. Unmercifully, he had ripped from her eyes the veil of innocence, and not even the torrent of tears she had shed could wash away the humiliation of his scornful rejection. A *child*, he had called her . . . was always calling her . . . but no more! His actions had destroyed the foolish child whose adoration and desire to serve had demonstrated her infatuation. With his help she had weathered the painful process of growing up, and now she felt free, free of his dominance, free of her fear of him, and best of all free of the fascination that had made her a slave to the whims of an unfeeling monster!

"I'd like to go with you to the caves, Robin," she decided coolly. "Will today be convenient?"

Robin's glance sharpened, wondering at the absence of the diffidence she usually displayed in her husband's presence. "My God, you have changed!" he breathed, before taking up the challenge. "I'll be delighted to have your company any time, Hazel, you know that."

"Can I go too?" Carmen was already sliding from her chair, sure of her answer, but Hazel stopped her.

"No, dear, I'm feeling rather tired, but as your uncle is so insistent I should rest, I feel sure he won't mind amusing you for the rest of today while I enjoy a leisurely tour of the caves." Catryn's open-mouthed astonishment was comical and even Carmen's re-

proaches died a silent death at the enormity of the suggestion, but Hazel met Francisco's arrogantly upswept head without concern. He allowed the silence to stretch to breaking point, pinning her in his sights as if determined to break her apathy by sheer force of will, but when her expression did not alter he conceded narrowly:

"Very well, a few more swimming lessons will not come amiss. Perhaps, Catryn, as my wife is to be otherwise occupied, you would like to join us?" Catryn accepted with uncertain pleasure, not caring for the way in which events were shaping. It had suited her well to see Hazel cowering in the shadow of a dictatorial husband, but her abrupt *volte-face* had affected him curiously. Although quick to recover, his first reaction had been one of amazement – the amazement of a master whose dog had suddenly turned and bitten him!

Hazel stood up, completely in command, and informed Robin as she pushed back her chair, "I'll fetch my wrap. Meet me outside when you're ready."

They drove almost in silence through typical Majorcan farmland, along a road bordered on both sides by almond trees in full blossom. Gradually the pink and white perfumed petals gave way to thick-topped fig trees and as they drove through a village on a hill, they passed an old restored mill, with vanes and sunshades, serving as a bar and resting place. They swooped down the hill towards a small harbour full of small boats nestling within the shelter of cliffs. On one side was a sprawling white-walled residence which might have housed a noble family but which was in reality the very exclusive residents' yacht club, and on

the other a small picturesque settlement of houses and shops perched either side of narrow streets rising steeply from the harbour. Hazel would have liked to linger there, but he drove straight on. "We'll stop on the way back for lunch at the yacht club," he promised, reading her look of disappointment. "Few tourists find this place – too far off the beaten track – but the organized parties allowed by Francisco are brought to the caves in coaches at the same time and on the same days each week. Unfortunately, today is one of those days, that's why I don't want to linger. Your first visit to the caves will be one you'll remember always, and if there's just the two of us present you'll savour the first glorious impact to the full."

"Thoughtful Robin!" She patted his hand, then withdrew into solitary thought. Her over-strained emotions could not cope with casual conversation, but happily he understood and did not intrude further, so that it was in quite a happy frame of mind that she stepped out of the car on to a bare piece of ground and looked around for some sign to guide her.

"This way." He took her arm and led her towards a path cutting through grassy banks. At first the ground ran level, then gradually it began to slope until the banks were far overhead and the path in front dipped into a tomb of darkness. "Take it slowly," he advised, his grasp tightening as she stumbled. "There's a switch inside the caves – somewhere around here, I think." He grunted satisfaction when his groping hand found a lever, then after a click their path was illuminated by lights cunningly concealed behind formations of glistening, golden-coloured rock. "Francisco em-

ployed experts to do the lighting. I think it has paid off, don't you?"

Robin smiled when she did not answer, remembering his own first excursion into the world of hidden beauty. Hazel was gazing upwards, reverently, as befitted the majestic atmosphere inside nature's own private cathedral. Thrusting downward from the high domed roof were immense stalactites, mighty spears of golden stone dripping water the colour of honey into pools secretly illuminated a clear, crystal blue. Upwards from the pools, their tips seemingly striving to pierce the surface were matching stalagmites grouped closely together to resemble giants of oak and cedar, a breathtaking underwater forest of stone undisturbed for centuries except for drips of water sliding tears of loneliness down the massive columns, carving beauty out of stone on their descent towards the pool.

The path wound erratically, first right, then left, disclosing around each crooked corner further masterpieces fashioned by nature out of stone and water; inanimate animal figures; religious images – the cowl-shrouded figure of a monk with head bent in silent prayer – the brass pipes of an organ; even a bunch of orange-red carrots to scoff dubious minds too attuned to reality to accept as genuine nature's impish flights of fancy. "See how the lights accentuate the colour of the stone?" Robin pointed, directing her eyes upwards towards a flag of many colours, striped orange and yellow with a fringe of deep red, unfurled against a background of wax white. "And there!" he pointed again. "Sheets hung out to dry!" He projected excited admiration of the men whose labours had resulted in

the exact spotlighting of shapes to render them even more visible, the precise pointing of light that helped stalactites assume perfect form; the tracing with light the course of meandering streams; and the probing of deep pools unwilling to voluntarily reveal their secrets.

"It's unbelievable!" she whispered, catching a breath as the cavern widened into a second wider cave shelved with stone seats to resemble an amphitheatre, its stage a wide sweep of blue lagoon upon which floated a solitary canoe bearing the hunched-up figure of a man.

"Sit here a moment," Robin smiled. "He's an entertainer laid on especially for the benefit of the tourists, but if I explain who you are I'm sure he'll be delighted to give you a solo performance."

Hazel did not know quite what to expect when she sat down to wait, but she did not mind lingering in such surroundings. Craning her neck upwards, she followed the outline of colossal columns, then shivered, wondering how such a world of frozen objects would react upon the nerves of a solitary wanderer. The Cuevas del Drach, when glowing with light, were palaces of enchantment, but there were crevices deep and dark where a monster might lurk waiting, in the manner of its namesake, for darkness to act as cover for his crimes . . . !

She did not realize how tense she had become until the strains of a violin began straying across the water. When Robin rejoined her she relaxed upon the stone bench and watched the violinist drifting in his boat across the blue lake, coaxing soft, beautiful music from the strings of his violin. Robin's arm was supporting her waist and when he pulled her closer her weary

head drooped against his shoulder.

"Something tells me you've had it tough, honey," he growled.

"Shush! Don't spoil it by talking," Hazel admonished dreamily. For a further few minutes they listened while music breathed life into an Eden of stone, then the boat drifted out of sight until all that remained was a faint echo of magic.

"Gee," Robin sighed, "I wish Jenny could have heard that! Music needs to be shared with a compatible soul to be fully appreciated and, like you, she becomes lost to the world when the music, the atmosphere, and the company in which she finds herself all hit exactly the right note."

"Jenny?" she queried, still haunted by the wonderful sound.

"My girl," he admitted sheepishly. "We're getting married when I get back home."

Shaking herself free of lingering nostalgia, but still a little enchanted, she smiled, "How wonderful! I'm so pleased for you, Robin – it must be heavenly to be so much in love."

"Don't you know?" he questioned sharply, suspicions aroused.

He sensed her recoil from the question, but her voice was cool as rain when she reminded him lightly, "But of course, I married Francisco, didn't I?"

Conscious of her resentment of his unthinking probing, he released her, but then, impelled by her obvious unhappiness, he offered, "If ever you should need anyone, let me know, Hazel! Promise . . . ?"

She stood up, dismissing emotion with a shrug. "I'm

not a child, I'll carve out my own destiny, thank you."
She laughed coolly, astonishing him with her newly-discovered wisdom, feeling suddenly confident within the protective shell that had been tailored to her individual requirements by a man whose indifference cut like a blade. Robin recognized heartbreak behind the glint of reckless defiance; something or someone had hurt her so deeply she was physically numbed and he felt compassion and a desire to be at hand to help her overcome the agony in store when time began reviving the nerve-ends of severed emotions . . .

"Let's go for lunch!" he decided, startling her with the abrupt decision.

"Lovely!" Her smile was as forced as her reply, but he pretended not to notice and began leading the way, guiding her footsteps along a crumbling path edged with boulders until a small ring of daylight appeared ahead. Once above ground sunlight exploded into eyes become accustomed to dimness and they blinked rapidly until they were able to focus normally. Harvest flies buzzed lazily in the heat, the sky was a blue sea devoid of movement except for a brassy ball of sun slowly traversing its surface. "I'd love a swim before lunch," she confessed, wishing she had had the foresight to bring along a costume.

"Plenty of shops down by the harbour," Robin offered, reading the problem correctly. "And what's more, an acquaintance of mine has offered me the loan of his yacht, so what say we take up his offer and go for a sail? We could buy a couple of costumes and swim later when lunch has had time to be digested." To skim across the hot sea with white sails grabbing every

available puff of wind seemed to her a heavenly idea, so she nodded enthusiastic support. "Right!" He threw back his lion's mane of hair and laughed, displaying a throat of bronze rising from the open collar of his white shirt. "We'll play hookey, and to hell with the consequences!"

Lunch at the yacht club was made all the more enjoyable by the atmosphere of stolen pleasure affected by their decision to play truant. Robin should have worked at least part of the day, and Hazel felt blithely unconcerned at the thought of Francisco's reaction to her prolonged absence. They ate *lechoncillo*, roast sucking pig, which she thought was delicious until she caught sight of the pathetic little corpse lying on a huge platter. Robin teased her unmercifully about her scruples, but ordered a *paella* cooked with a variety of seafood, chicken and vegetables and served on a bed of saffron rice, which she found so enjoyably filling she could manage nothing afterwards except coffee. For an hour they lazed on the shaded terrace, then reluctantly they abandoned their leisure to go in search of costumes and towels. These were purchased with the minimum of effort from a shop on the quayside, together with a yachting cap for her and one for Robin with a nautical badge and peak, which she insisted upon buying. "As a thank-you for a wonderful day," she pleaded when he waved her money away. "Please, Robin, – you're the only one for whom I feel able to buy a present – even Carmen's toys are the most expensive money can buy."

The simple explanation touched him on the raw; it said so much, yet left so much unsaid. "Sweet, adorable Nut-brown," he said gruffly, his merry eyes moment-

arily grave. "Very well, I accept with pleasure, but only on condition that you let me buy you a memento in return?"

She hesitated. Robin never seemed short of money and he was generous to a fault, but a costly gift would be sure to arouse comment at the Casa. However, she could hardly refuse without causing offence. "I'd love a fan." She seized a cheap paper one hanging from a string outside the doorway of the shop. He took it and replaced it without a second look.

"And a fan you shall have," he promised, a glint in his eye promising argument if she should protest, "but one of my choice, if you don't mind – I'm very particular about the presents I give to my girl-friends."

Her heart sank, but knowing protest would be useless, she allowed him to lead her up one of the narrow shop lined streets until they came to a jewellers, its windows crammed to capacity with costly chess sets of ivory, watches set with diamonds, gold bracelets, pendants and rings set with every available choice of stone. It was a surprise to find such a shop in a tiny harbour town, but Robin's greeting to the proprietor dispelled some of her curiosity.

"*Buenos dias, señor* – your establishment has been recommended to me by some friends back in the States. They reckon you trade almost exclusively with American tourists who, as is well known, don't quibble about paying out a few extra bucks if they know they're getting a genuine bargain."

"That is correct, *señor*," the dignified Spaniard responded to Robin's cheery grin. "German and American tourists form the majority of our customers.

He shrugged apologetically, guessing Hazel's nationality. "However, *señor*, you can be happy with the thought that whatever goods you acquire will cost you far less than they would in your own country."

"Does that salve your conscience, honey?" he quirked a sandy eyebrow, amused by her wide-eyed diffidence. "Whatever we buy will be cheap at the price, so forget about scruples and choose whatever you fancy." But she had eyes only for a showcase of beautiful fans spread out behind glass upon a background of crimson velvet. The artistry and workmanship put into the fashioning of the dainty pieces was breathtaking – some were made of black lace intricately woven into a variety of patterns, some had diamond-studded spokes and others were painted with flowers or views of local scenery. To choose was an impossible task, but Robin had no hesitation in pointing out his preference. "What about this one?" he indicated. "It's you somehow – pale, slender, and delicately lovely."

"*No!*" Hazel stepped back, surprising him with her vehemence. "Not pearls, and not ivory – if you don't mind, I'll have the little green one with the painted flowers."

When the proprietor turned a gasp into a cough Robin's eyebrows rose, but he instructed calmly, "You heard the lady, *señor*, the little green one it is."

They left with the proprietor's good wishes ringing in their ears, Hazel clutching the fan to her breast, hardly able to wait until she could examine it more closely and to gloat over its beauty. It was the most exciting present she had ever received – her first from a man, if one excluded Francisco's presents, which

were more in the nature of heirlooms on loan – and already she loved it. Cost did not matter, she treasured the trinket more for the kindness of its donor than for its negligible monetary value.

Afterwards, the sail came as an anticlimax, a wonderful experience and an enjoyable one, but soon to become just a hazy memory. Little persuasion was needed by Robin to coax her into joining him for dinner, then later, on the terrace of his hotel, they danced to records and shared drinks and small talk with the other residents. It was well past midnight when he deposited her at the door of the Casa. Only one light was burning, the one in Francisco's study, so Robin made no protest when she urged him on his way.

"Thank you for a glorious day." She leant across the door of his open-top tourer, digging the toes of her slippers into the gravel of the drive, and smiled at him as he leant forward on the steering wheel.

He smiled wryly, thinking how rarely his dates ended in platonic goodbyes.

"I enjoyed it too, honey, but run along now before I forget both my girl-friend and the husband you have hovering somewhere in the background!" Her startled look made him regret his thoughtless attempt to amuse – her shell of confidence was deceiving, underneath she was still the same timid creature whose wide-eyed belief in her husband's ability to control the elements had wrung his heart. A half-smile of uncertainty lifted the corner of her mouth, then to his delight she bent to feather a kiss upon his cheek before spinning round to run hastily up the steps and into the

Casa. She raced up the stairs without a glance towards the door behind which she knew Francisco was waiting and did not stop until she gained the safety of her room where, once inside, she turned the key in the lock of her bedroom door – and also the one adjoining.

CHAPTER XI

NEXT day Hazel remained in her room until she was sure Francisco had left for the factory. Shutting her ears to the sound of Carmen's piping voice demanding admittance, she remained silent until, thinking she was still asleep, the child moved away. Her disconsolate footsteps retreating down the passageway gave Hazel a few bad moments, but she promised herself that once Francisco's car had headed down the drive she would seek Carmen out and make it up to her by allowing her to follow any pursuit she wished for the rest of the day. It was a cowardly action, the confrontation would have to be faced some time, but a few hours' respite from his scathing questions was a prospect soothing to her uneasy conscience.

It was after ten when she went downstairs. Coffee was brewing in the dining salon and rolls had been left in a covered dish, so after assuring a hovering servant that she wanted nothing more, she ate a frugal breakfast then went in search of Carmen. She was in the grounds playing ball with Tio Garcia whose relief at the sight of her was obvious. "*Gracias a Dios!*" he exclaimed, wiping the back of his hand across a perspiring forehead. "Much as I adore the company of this delightful child, her energy can become trying after a time! Take over for me if you will, *cara*, while I totter along to drape my ancient bones across the nearest seat."

"Let me help you," Hazel gurgled, pandering to his

theatrical gestures of infirmity. "Poor Tio, you look ready to drop!" He allowed them both to escort him to a garden seat, his groans of despair sending Carmen into shrieks of laughter, then once settled he abandoned pretence and surveyed them both with a benign twinkle.

"Oh, Tio, you are fun!" Carmen giggled. "Will you stay with us for the rest of today?"

"Actually, I came to invite you out. I thought as Hazel's tour of the factory was curtailed we might return to visit the showrooms – a sight too interesting to be missed."

"Thank you, Tio . . . but not today, if you don't mind," Hazel stammered, striving to think up an excuse with which to soften the bald refusal.

"Just as you wish," he shrugged, his expression bland. "It was a mere whim thought up to amuse you during Francisco's absence, but I won't press you if you don't wish to go."

"Francisco's absence?" she queried uncertainly.

"His trip to Formentor on the far side of the island, surely he must have mentioned it? Considering it will be very late when he returns I think it most remiss of him if he has not."

"Perhaps he did mention it . . . yes, I'm sure he must have, probably it slipped my memory." Tio Garcia's grave smile hid concern; he was not one whit deceived by her white lie but he played up, knowing she wished to avoid the danger of Carmen becoming a martyr to insecurity through sensing constant dissension between the adult members of her family.

"I love the factory," Carmen appealed wistfully,

"there's so much to look at. Last time we were there I was allowed to pack some brooches into special boxes and the lady who helped me said they were to be despatched the very next day all the way to New York."

"Then let's find out if they've gone, shall we?" Hazel suggested, turning bright eyes from Carmen to Tio and being rewarded by instant grins of pleasure.

When they arrived production was in full swing, so they skirted the main buildings and made towards the showroom which stood apart, its frontage emblazoned with the name famous all over the world for the quality of its products. Inside, the long, one-storied building was set out like a store, with glass-topped counters displaying pearl ornaments of every description. Each counter was devoted to separate items, rings, brooches and necklaces, and pleasant salesgirls able to converse in several languages were ready with answers to the many questions put to them by the tourists. As they wandered around, Carmen kept up a flow of chatter which Tio Garcia coped with amiably so that Hazel might concentrate upon her enjoyment of the many pieces on show behind the barriers of glass. Her sharp ears picked up the conversation of two American ladies nearby. "I swear, Moira," one was assuring the other, "my Harry paid thousands for this string I'm wearing. He'll never believe me when I tell him how impossible it is to tell the difference between my pearls and these imitations!"

Carmen tugged at Tio Garcia's sleeve. "If our pearls are imitation, where do real ones come from?" she queried.

"Legend has it that they were first found in the sea

of Japan," he informed her whimsically. "One night a beautiful princess and her lover were kept apart by the gods of evil on the banks of Ago Bay in Japan. The queen of the night was so unhappy at the sight of the distressed couple that she shed many, many tears. As her teardrops fell from the black heavens they were covered by the glow from the full moon and dropped into the sea to become pearls." The tale caught at Hazel's heart. It was appropriate that the bridal suite of the Casa should be crammed with pearls, frozen teardrops of a legion of unhappy women unfortunate enough to have fallen under the dark spell of the men of Drach.

"Is it true, Hazel, or is Tio Garcia just teasing?" Carmen demanded, uncertain whether or not to believe.

Forced into the role of oracle, Hazel flashed Tio Garcia an apologetic look before explaining, "As Tio said, it is legend, and legends are stories repeated to generation after generation until fact becomes distorted by fiction and no one is quite sure how much is truth and how much a figment of someone's imagination."

"But some of it *might* be true?" she persisted, not wanting to disbelieve Tio Garcia's froth of romantic nonsense.

"A very tiny part, perhaps," Hazel compromised.

"Tut, tut!" Tio Garcia pretended to scold. "Leave the child to her dreams, if she wants to believe in fairy tales then why not let her?"

"Because it is wrong to allow a child to grow up believing everything and everyone in the world is perfect! There are no gallant knights on white chargers,

no fairy godmothers to change wishes into reality," she rounded, surprising him with a glimpse of bitter hurt. "Common sense is more rewarding than daydreams, at least if one is taught to be cautious it lessens the chances of being hurt!" When Tio Garcia's shocked dismay registered, she apologized immediately, "I'm sorry, Tio, that was no way to reward your kindness. Please forgive me."

When Carmen moved out of earshot, he answered quietly, "I feel it is I who should apologize to you, *cara*, on my nephew's behalf. I had hoped that in time you two would move towards a better understanding, you have so much that he needs and, though you may scoff at the suggestion, he has it in him him to make some-one happy if only he can be shown the way. However, if as I suspect, it is he who is responsible for your disillusionment, then I shall find it very hard to forgive him."

His amazement knew no bounds when she defended, "No, Tio, don't desert him, he must have *someone*!"

"You feel that, too?" he seized eagerly upon her words. "I wish you could understand how much life is to blame for his unyielding exterior. Everyone he has ever loved has been taken from him; when he was just a few years old his father died, then his mother whom he adored, and later on his brother, the last remaining member of his family, was killed in the company of the only woman Francisco had ever loved. He must now be afraid to love, for to him, it has brought nothing but hurt, deprivation, and remorse, so who can blame him if he has decided never to allow himself to feel deeply about anyone ever again?"

Yesterday, she might have seized upon such vindication to excuse Francisco's actions, but today Tio Garcia's warm pleas made little impression on the icy casing protecting her heart. She shrugged her indifference and avoided an answer by changing the subject. "Tell me more about the pearls, Tio. Who decides upon colour, and why are there so many? Up until now I had imagined pearls to be predominantly white?"

With a sigh, he took the hint and did not try to force the issue. His voice lacked lustre when he began to explain, but his enthusiasm grew as he sensed her interest. "We take our lead from nature when deciding upon colour; each area where pearls are found produces a certain colour of pearl. The finest pink and cream-coloured gem pearls grow inside a small oyster found in the Persian Gulf and these command the highest price of all natural pearls. Large silver-white ones called 'silver lips' are produced in the northern waters of Australia; dark and black pearls in the black-shelled oysters along the Pacific coast of Mexico, and pink ones are found in the queen conch of the West Indies. Colour, you see, is influenced by the temperature of the water in which the oyster lives, as well as by the state of the oyster's life and the food it digests."

Nodding at a smiling salesgirl, he leant across a showcase and picked up a brooch from under the glass. It was shaped out of gold into the likeness of a mermaid, a slim golden body tapering into a tail of rubies with fins set in diamonds and a burst of unevenly-shaped pearls rising like bubbles from tail to head. "We also strive for authenticity in the matter of shape," he pointed to the pearl bubbles. "Sometimes pearls become lodged in

the oysters' muscular tissue and are moulded by the pressures of the tough muscle fibres to produce an irregular shape similar to these which are known as baroque pearls. Everything is manufactured as closely as possible to the real thing, but naturally, as the demand is greater, emphasis is placed more upon the production of perfect articles rather than the copying of nature's freaks."

Replacing the brooch, he smiled his thanks to the salesgirl and they moved on. He excelled as a guide when he put his mind to it, and with so enthralled a pupil he was doubly encouraged, stopping at each showcase to explain the various shapes and designs into which the pearls were incorporated and betraying at the same time an enthusiasm and love for the pearl's history. "You have great knowledge of your subject, Tio," she admired, as they halted before a tapestry covering the whole of one wall depicting the Hindu god Krishna, bedecked with pearls to protect him from death, going into battle with a snake. "I had no idea the gem was discovered so far back in time."

"Indeed, yes," he affirmed. "Old Indian legends of the creation of the world show that the pearl was associated with love and gentleness. They say that in the beginning when the great god created air, fire, earth and water, each of the elements gave him a gift. The air gave him a rainbow to form a halo about his head; fire gave him a meteor to light his way; earth gave him a ruby to decorate his forehead and the water gave him a pearl to wear over his heart. That is why in the East they believe that the pearl is a gift from the gods." His attention was attracted by a wave from

Carmen, who was happily engaged trying on rings in a vain effort to find one to fit her small finger, so he missed the shadow that clouded Hazel's face. To her, pearls could never be associated with love and gentleness, quite the reverse. Symbols of heartbreak perhaps, trappings of wealth seized upon by men with too little imagination to recognise the irony of bestowing tear-gems upon their unhappy wives. Within the pearl-decorated bridal chamber, secreted behind her pillow, lay the only offering she had ever been given in a spirit of gentle kindness – the little green fan which she valued far in excess of the remote, priceless possessions conferred as a sop to duty.

A voice reached her through her absorption – an echo from a nightmare which she ignored, hoping it would fade into obscurity. "Your late night has not tired you as much as your absence at breakfast this morning seemed to imply." There was bite in the voice and a thread of irony running through the words. Next to her Tio Garcia stiffened, then, his surprise obviously genuine, he swung round to greet his nephew. "Francisco! Was I mistaken in thinking that today you were to have visited Formentor?"

"You were not," Francisco corrected, interpreting in Hazel's mute white face signs of dismay. "At the last moment my business meeting had to be postponed. An attempt was made to contact me at the Casa before I left, but I was already on my way when they telephoned. Once I arrived at Formentor and was acquainted with the news I returned immediately."

"Surely you could have remained long enough to have lunch!" Tio Garcia protested. "One drive along

those mountain tracks is bad enough without adding to the burden by tackling a return journey without rest or refreshment!" He did not look tired, his eyes were narrowed, not yet adjusted to freedom from spearing sun, and his mouth was sternly unrelaxed, suggesting hidden springs of tension. Hazel's eyes were upon his hands as he chose a cheroot from a slim case and astonishment swept through her when the tense fingers bit into a brown stem with such force that tobacco spilled in a mangled heap at his feet. Hazel looked up and quivered when she met the blast from his brooding eyes, then felt sudden anxiety when she sensed the supreme effort brought to bear to make his voice sound negligent when he answered.

"I had other urgent business here which I had thought to put off but which, on reflection, I decided was best accomplished with all urgency." Although he did not say what business it was, she felt in some way connected, and when he smiled, a thin widening of the lips to show teeth instant white before it faded, she knew how a prisoner must feel as he stands before a firing squad – terrified, helpless and devoid of all hope.

The atmosphere was too intense to be comfortable, and Tio Garcia's brow furrowed as he suggested, "It might be as well if I took Hazel and the child back to the Casa – the heat is becoming trying and Hazel is not yet fully acclimatized."

She did feel stifled, her hands were clammy with sweat and trickles of moisture were running between her shoulder blades. If Francisco had suggested accompanying them she would have run – anywhere, but preferably into the cool sea to seek escape from the

heat of his dragon's breath, but to her relief he nodded agreement of the plan, thereby postponing for a short interval the confrontation which she knew was certain to erupt between them before the sun had risen on another day.

Later that evening he sent a servant with a message that he was waiting for her in his study. She was sitting in her room playing idly with the little green fan, running her fingers along its smooth spokes and admiring the figures painted with delicate, colourful precision against a background of tightly stretched silk. She had dined early with Carmen, then when the child had been bedded down for the night she had retreated to her own room to enjoy a welcome shower before retiring at an hour incomprehensible to Spaniards, whose customary afternoon siesta enabled them to stretch their evenings into the early hours of the following day. Nervously she tightened the belt of her flower-patterned dressing gown around her slim waist, then still clutching the fan in tense fingers, she made her way downstairs.

He was lounging in an armchair, his head resting against blue velvet upholstery, his long slim-trousered legs thrust forward allowing him to study glistening shoe leather with brooding absorption. He rose to his feet when she entered and sauntered across to pour drinks from a tray containing crystal decanters glowing wine deep under the light of brilliant chandeliers. Hazel ignored the wine he placed on a nearby table and sought a chair to support her trembling limbs. For a long while there was silence, then he spoke from the depths of his armchair.

"You know, of course, that I am extremely angry — and why."

She gulped in air. "Yes, I know why. You're angry because I spent the whole of yesterday with Robin."

"All day and practically *all night*!" he jerked out viciously, anger rising at the coolness of her reply. She jumped to her feet; although panic was beating like a wild thing in her breast she had no intention of being made the victim of vindictive rage. She had almost reached the door when he pounced, trapping her shoulders in a grip of steel. "I will not allow it, do you hear? Never again will you bring dishonour upon my name by spending hours alone in the company of another man!"

"Why not, for heaven's sake!" Her indignation was so great she could barely choke out the words. "What's so wrong about wanting to be with a friend, a dear friend, one with whom I have shared the only happy hours I've known since coming to this island!" Her hand flew to her mouth, shocked at having put into words a thought which until then had lurked dormant in a dark corner of her heart. But it was too late to wish the words unsaid. His skin seemed stretched over features clamped with ungovernable emotion when he flung her from him and thrust clenched fists out of sight, as if he could barely trust himself to control an urge to tighten them around the young neck rising defiantly from a collar of ruffled silk. He took a step backward and lifted his glass from the table to lift it in a savage toast. "Then join me in a toast to your absent friend!"

His glittering satisfaction caused her a shiver of

suspicion. "Why *absent* friend? So far as I am aware Robin is just a few miles from here?"

"So far as you are aware," he mocked, suddenly mellow. Satisfaction played around his mouth as he followed up, "By this time I imagine your friend will be well on his way to Los Angeles. His company were informed by me earlier today that if they wished to finish their work in the caves they would have to replace Carstair immediately. They did not hesitate. He was instructed to return on the first available flight, and if he is wise he will never set foot on this island again!"

His wild brand of justice was shocking. She stared at him, glimpsing the monster behind a façade of culture, and in her agitation began folding and unfolding the fan with quick, mechanical jerks. "How could you?" she whispered. "Robin's job meant so much to him – you had no right to deprive him of it simply to avenge unfounded suspicion."

He gave an easy shrug. "So far as I am concerned he may work anywhere his company care to send him, with one exception," he tossed back his wine with relish, then spat: "*here!*" When he lowered his glass his eyes alighted upon the fan she was holding to her breast as if it were a talisman against evil. "Where did you get that?" he queried, plucking it from her grasp before she had time to realize his intention. Finding no reason to lie, she told him:

"Robin bought it for me yesterday, just an inexpensive present to remind me of a wonderful day."

Francisco flicked it open, casting it only one glance before snapping it closed.

"Jade, gold, and hand-painted silk, *inexpensive?*" he

jarred through clenched teeth. "*Sacramento!* what kind of a fool do you take me for?" Before her disbelieving eyes the fan was thrown on to the carpet and ground under his heel with a sickening crunch that spelt destruction to its fragile loveliness.

"You beast!" she cried, dropping to her knees with a sob to try to salvage something out of the mangled remains. Nursing the debris in gentle hands, she raised her head to meet his arrogant stare and the last particle of hope within her died. "I'm leaving," she told him with expressionless finality. "Our marriage must be annulled – I was a fool to let you talk me into it."

He speared over her to denounce, "Not as great a fool as I was, *amada*, when I convinced myself that innocence could exist even though your quick acceptance of material benefits made nonsense of the thought. You were bought, remember? And until such time as I think fit, you will remain here and carry out the duties you were employed to do."

Bought! She flinched from his callous use of the word. "I won't stay," she forced out desperately, white to the lips. "If I decide to leave there's no way you can stop me!"

He swung away, aggravated by her attitude of despair as she knelt at his feet, her head bowed over the broken remains of the treasured fan. His voice reached her clearly, clamped words spoken with such icy detachment there could be no doubt he meant what he said. "If you go, Carmen must go too. I am tired of complications, of constant female bickering. There is a convent school on the mainland which can accommodate her immediately, so when you do decide to

leave let me know and I'll arrange transport for you both." He left the room without a backward glance at the kneeling figure staring through tear-filled eyes at the pieces of fan cradled in her cupped hands, but he must have known he left her shattered, with heart and hopes ground to pieces under the weight of his blatant blackmail.

CHAPTER XII

FOR days afterwards Hazel found it easy to keep out of Francisco's way. Each morning after breakfast his car drove away in the direction of the factory and did not return until evening long after dinner, sometimes after everyone in the Casa had retired to bed. She could not sleep on these occasions, but lay awake for hours seeking escape from the trap enclosing her, her determination to break free accelerated by the knowledge that Francisco was finding consolation in the company of Catryn, who had once made plain her willingness to play the role of comforter. The days dragged almost as wearily as the nights. Carmen's company and Tio's solicitude helped in a small way, but not enough to ease the burden which grew daily heavier, causing her small face to become pinched and her ready smile to disappear almost completely from a mouth that suffered wild periods of uncontrollable trembling.

Tio Garcia was disturbed. He had watched with heartache the change in his now much-loved niece, and Francisco's prolonged absences had also been noted and shrewdly assessed. The rift between the two was wide and growing wider. Something, he decided, would have to be done.

"Has Francisco mentioned that he has a house in Palma?" he questioned idly as they shared a seat in the grounds watching Carmen playing on a swing Hazel had had erected on the branch of a huge tree.

Hazel quivered as she always did at the sound of his name, but strove to answer casually. "No, he's never mentioned it."

"It's a beautiful house," he enthused, hoping to strike an answering spark. "When his mother was alive it was used frequently, but for the past few years it has been ignored, so much so that it worries me." Her head lifted, betraying fractional interest, and he felt encouraged to continue, "It's not that I distrust the servants – the resident housekeeper and her husband have been in the family's employ for years and are thoroughly trustworthy – but a house needs people; without them it grows cold and shows signs of neglect." He felt the choosing of his words was a touch of genius; any subject pertaining to neglect was sure to arouse her sympathy.

"What a pity!" she sighed, then upon reflection. "I'd like to see it, Tio – would it be possible, do you think?"

Curbing his eagerness, he suggested, "Why don't we spend a few days there? You have yet to visit our capital, and Carmen also will find much there to amuse her." Wisely he did not prod her into an immediate decision, but lapsed into silence, giving her time to savour the proposition. His patience was rewarded when finally she half-agreed.

"I'd like that very much, but I doubt if Francisco will allow us to leave the Casa, and I certainly couldn't bring myself to ask his permission."

"Leave that to me, *cara*," he told her, his usually kind mouth stern. "I'll speak to him this evening and, all being well, we can look forward to a welcome change

of scenery within the next few days."

No mention was made by Tio Garcia of what passed between them, but Francisco must have agreed, because a week later they were established in Palma, the city created initially by the nobility of Majorca in order to seek respite from the solitude of their country estates in splendid residences built with pleasure and entertaining in mind. On their way to the house they passed through parts of the city still retaining an appearance of former centuries, with narrow streets, pointed arches and sloping roofs, before driving into a square set apart from the main thoroughfare. The car swung through stone pillars supporting massive gates swung wide open in welcome, then entered a courtyard where fountains splashed coolly into stone basins and trees and shrubs planted in large stone pots thrived under shaded archways and marched in single file up stone steps and along the fretted ironwork balustrade leading upwards into the house.

Hazel's heart sank when they entered a magnificent reception room, its walls lined from floor to ceiling with priceless tapestries. A huge chandelier admired its own reflection in a gilt-framed mirror hung above a marble fireplace, and a line of brass-studded chairs were sternly regimented as if to discourage use by all but the elegantly poised. She had imagined a smaller house with comfortable rooms and well used furniture, a place where she could cast off memories and start afresh, but instead here was just another awe-inspiring pile packed with the trappings of wealthy nobility to remindly her of the man she was trying so unsuccessfully to forget.

"Are you disappointed?" Tio Garcia sounded anxious.

"Of course not," she assured him hastily, "it's just that it's rather overwhelming at first sight." He smiled his relief, then, obviously more than ready for his usual siesta, he left them in the housekeeper's hands and withdrew to his room.

Carmen loved Palma, especially the horse-drawn carriages which she rode in at every possible opportunity, the fascinating shops, the busy port with its succession of ocean-going liners spilling tourists on to the island, and the airport where Tio Garcia took them to lunch in the restaurant and where throughout the meal he manfully suffered the noise of screaming jet engines and Carmen's spasmodic excursions from table to balcony to watch planes alternately landing or taking off. In one respect he was typical of his race, he liked to enjoy his food in relaxing surroundings, so when a pucker appeared between his eyes and he pushed away his plate with uncharacteristic peevishness Hazel realized his patience was wearing thin. He was so willing to show them around, so chivalrously determined to escort them everywhere, it was hard to remember that his tall figure owed a lot of its slenderness to old age. She reached out to enclose his strumming fingers within her cool grasp.

"You're tired, Tio, why not go home and rest? Carmen will resist being dragged away from here for another hour at least!"

He shook his head. "No, I wouldn't dream of it. I would be failing in my duty to you both."

"Nonsense!" she derided crisply, worried about the

way he flinched each time an engine began to whine. "Palma is full of tourists, people of my own nationality in whose company I feel completely at ease. No harm could possibly come to us, but if only to put your mind at rest, I'll promise to take a taxi home once we're ready to leave." He would not have given in even then had not an announcer boomed that the arrival of a jumbo jet was imminent. He paled, obviously unable to bear the idea of enduring a still greater increase in decibels, then capitulated.

"If you're sure you don't mind . . ."

Hazel was as content as Carmen to remain on the balcony of the restaurant watching people of all nations arriving and departing in streamlined aircraft that swooped, dipped and glided through the sky, landing and taking off with the confidence of graceful birds. But even pleasure can pall, so after a while they left the balcony and made their way downstairs in search of an exit. The lounges were crowded with passengers either newly arrived or waiting to depart; loudspeakers boomed flight information and added to the uproar created by hundreds of voices seeking information, directions, or simply reassurance. They fought their way through the crush to the taxi rank, and Hazel was just about to hail a car when a familiar voice shattered her tranquillity.

"Don't bother, I'll take you wherever you want to go."

"Tio Francisco!" Carmen sounded half pleased, half dismayed, "we thought you were still at the Casa."

He addressed Carmen, but Hazel felt his explanation was directed to herself. "I came to the airport to meet

a business acquaintance, but for some reason his flight has been delayed, which means I am left with at least three hours to fill before the plane is due to land."

She could think of nothing to say. He seemed slightly less aloof than usual, less unbending, and in her search for a reason she seized at once upon boredom as the compulsion behind his offer of a lift. Perversely, she decided the day was too young and the weather too warm to be bearable indoors.

"Thank you," she refused politely, "but we're not ready to go back just yet. I promised Carmen we would pay another visit to the harbour."

She hated the bland amusement behind his smile; he seemed determined to triumph over her on every possible occasion, and this was to be no exception. "Good," his thumb pressed down to release the catch on the car door. "Get in, I'll take you."

The fast car transported them swiftly from the airport into Palma, driving straight through the Borne, the main promenade lined with cafés, bars and entertainment halls, until he reached a quiet old harbour with on one side a view of shipping docks and quays and on the other a breathtaking panorama of vast bay. She left the car reluctantly and began sauntering along a path which at one time had formed the jetty of the harbour and as the sun warmed her body her heart warmed also to the beauty and peace of her surroundings. He caught her up and shortened his stride to drop into step beside her. Carmen had raced on ahead, and her pink-frocked figure could just be seen in the distance waiting for them to catch up, but he beckoned her back until she stood panting before him.

"Why can't I go on ahead?" she pouted, ready to battle for her rights.

Instead of the usual scowl of impatience Hazel was expecting, he surprised them both by pointing down the jetty steps to where a brightly painted speedboat bobbed like a cork upon the water. "I thought you might prefer a trip in the *Mallorca Pearl*," he offered, his cheeks creasing into a grin that lifted Hazel's heart clear out of her breast. Boyish was an impossible description to apply even vaguely to the aristocratic Marqués, but the enthusiasm with which he helped them aboard, and his almost reverent touch upon the controls, bore marked resemblance to a schoolboy showing off a much prized toy.

"Is it really yours, Tio?" Carmen piped, scrambling over seats in an effort to see everything at once. He was heading the boat out into the open bay, breathing deeply of the cool air rushing past his face as he stood with feet apart, steadying the wheel. He turned to flash her a smile of enjoyment.

"Certainly it is, small one, would I be speeding it away from shore if it were not?"

"You might if you were a pirate!" she shouted back, entering thoroughly into the spirit of things. "You would make a good pirate, Tio, all big and fierce and brave!" When he threw back his head and laughed Hazel found herself in complete agreement; he had discarded his coat and constricting tie, and his white shirt, unbuttoned at the neck, left bare a brown column of throat rising to support a dark head of wind-tousled hair. Her heart contracted and she dug her nails fiercely into her palms, remembering the night she had

felt that strong throat pulsating wildly under her hands and the way his hair had brushed her cheek when strong emotion had strangled words of love from the man who had turned his back for ever on gentleness and affection. As the bows cut cleanly through the water, churning creamy spray against the sides of the boat, it was impossible not to feel exhilarated, then gradually as exhilaration grew it became even harder to remember that her companion was the same ruthless man who was using her love for Carmen to bind her to his side, a man who could crush fragility beneath his heel without the slightest compunction.

They sped out into the bay until land was a misty blur on the horizon, then he spun the wheel, turning a swift arc that left them gasping with excitement. "Would you like to take a turn at the wheel?" he shouted above the noise of the engine. She scrambled forward, her shining eyes reflecting golden with happiness, and was enclosed within the circle of his arms while he instructed her upon the use of the controls. The power beneath her hands felt frightening at first, but as his hands guided hers upon the wheel and his lips closed against her ear giving directions she became acutely conscious of his heart beating against the curve of her shoulder and the steel trap of muscled arms imprisoning her between himself and the wheel. Her hair was flying in the breeze, a rich chestnut veil that tickled his nose and whiplashed softly against his cheeks.

She was not prepared for the extra strain that ensued when he lifted a hand to clear his face, so that when the wheel spun in her hands, sending the boat completely off course, she screamed her helplessness. In less

than a second he had righted it, and as she sagged against him he began to laugh, such youthful, infectious laughter that they both had to join in, and as the boat's progress slowed to a lazy circle the sound of three voices echoed across the water, joining the calls of seabirds in carefree companionship.

After a while he cut the engine and allowed the boat to drift towards the shore while they relaxed in their seats and he took stock of their glowing faces. Under his scrutiny Hazel felt a blush rising. She looked away, shy of the change which she sensed was in some way deliberate, a well thought out action devised with a definite aim in mind. Carmen, however, had no scruples; she ran to clamber up on his knee and pleased him with the compliment, "I do like you today, Tio Francisco!"

A touch of wryness played around his mouth as he gazed down at his small niece. "Just today, *niña*? Not yesterday, and probably not tomorrow . . . ?"

She pursed her lips, then with a child's honesty admitted, "It depends . . . for many yesterdays you have been in scolding moods which have made Hazel and me very unhappy, but if every tomorrow can be like today then we will love you very much, won't we, Hazel?"

They waited for her answer, Carmen anxiously and Francisco with raised eyebrows and a muscle of amusement twitching beside his firm lips. Seeing her obviously lost for words, he eased her embarrassment by explaining:

"Adults are not so forgiving as children, *niña*; their hurt goes deeper and therefore is harder to forget."

With a glint of charm inherited from conquering ancestors, he enlisted Carmen's sympathy with an appeal for advice. "How does a gentleman best convince a lady of his intention to reform, do you think? The lady in question is kind but very suspicious of the gentleman's motives."

Hazel's eyes flew upwards to meet his and found gravity in place of the mockery she was expecting. Her heart lurched, realizing his words were the nearest approach he would ever make towards an apology. They showed one degree of pride less in the autocratic Marqués who had never before betrayed by even the flicker of an eyelid remorse for any of his misdeeds. Forgiveness stormed up inside her, but was suppressed. His twin destruction of her friendship with Robin and the fragile memento she had cherished for its beauty had cut too deeply into her heart to be healed by a salve of practised charm. His eyes were on her face as she pondered and remained there even when Carmen, who had been thinking long and deeply on the subject, delivered her verdict.

"I think the gentleman should try to make the lady like him by giving her presents of flowers and bonbons, then afterwards he could ask her to dinner, and if she agrees he should spend all his money on her to prove he values her friendship above all his possessions." She broke off, short of breath, and waited triumphantly for their reactions. Hazel looked dumbfounded, but Carmen was delighted when her uncle, after an initial twitch of amusement, paid her the compliment of taking her seriously.

"I think that's a splendid idea! Remind me to thank

you in more concrete form when next we pass a *tienda*."

They passed a sweetshop on their way home and he stopped the car to purchase the promised reward, two boxes of sweets which he solemnly presented, one to each, before restarting the car. He dropped them off at the house on his way to the airport, but when Carmen scrambled out to run to show Tio Garcia her present, Francisco caught hold of Hazel's wrist and delayed her long enough to question softly, "Is the child's advice worth following, do you think?"

"I've no idea what you mean," she side-stepped coolly, longing to escape but too proud to resist his detaining hand.

He glinted a warning that even now his patience might become strained, but then swallowed his pride and spelled out the invitation. "I'm asking you to dine with me this evening. There is a restaurant in the city which, besides serving very good food, has a dance floor and an excellent band."

A refusal sprang immediately to her lips, but was not voiced. Temptation was blotting out resentment and was urging her to take advantage of a mellow mood which tomorrow might disappear never to return. "Thank you," she gasped, feeling some invisible force prodding her into acceptance, then she snatched her wrist from out of his electrifying grasp and ran into the courtyard.

The new clothes had arrived from Madrid just a few hours before her departure from the Casa, so she had barely had time to skim through the wardrobe where they had been hung by a servant who had un-

packed the wealth of fabrics from out of their clouds of tissue paper. One dress in particular had caught her eye; it stood out from the rest because of its starkness of colour and because she knew it was not one of her choice but had been added to her list by someone whose taste differed widely from her own. It was black — sheer nylon filming over an underskirt dark as a forbidden dream, tight at the waist, with a skimming hipline widening gradually to a flared hem. Curiosity had impelled her to include it with the rest of her luggage, and as she prepared for her evening with Francesco she knew instinctively that the choice had been his.

That his taste was impeccable was borne out by her transformed image staring out of the mirror. Through sheer black nylon her arms and shoulders attained an untouched, virginal beauty; a diamanté belt, bracelet-wide, spanned her wisp of waist and slippers formed from slender straps of silver had matching diamanté around their soles so that when she moved rays of light flirted from gem to gem, adding elegance to her slender figure.

When he knocked upon her door she waited with confidence for him to enter. He was wearing a white dinner jacket and the corsage of tight crimson rosebuds he was carrying contrasted like drops of blood against his sleeve. He handed her the flowers, then stepped back a few paces to shape her figure with eyes inscrutable, missing nothing from the golden sheen of her hair to the nervous flexing of her toes in their trapping of silver. A lick of flame, quickly doused from his eyes, flared again in his voice as he helped her into her wrap and

invited softly: "Let's go!"

The restaurant was discreetly luxurious, catering almost exclusively for the local *aristocracia*. Panelling of dark wood gave to the interior an aura of antiquity which was emphasized by ornate chandeliers that glittered brilliantly above silver candelabra, gleaming cutlery and gilt-framed oil paintings of past dignitaries hung upon the walls. The murmur of small talk rising from the crowded tables ceased when they entered, and every eye was upon them as the head waiter escorted them to their table. The experience was not a pleasant one and had Francisco's hand not firmly propelled her forward she might have succumbed to the temptation to turn and run. Coolly, he returned stiff nods from men who seemed reluctant to acknowledge his presence. Their wives also were aloof, curiosity alone preventing them from dropping their eyes to avoid encountering his glance of glinting derision. Hazel was trembling by the time they reached their table, the unexpected hostility demoralizing her completely, but Francisco seemed completely unconcerned as he sat down to study a proffered wine list. A quartet of musicians began to play vigorously, as if they sensed the need to cover up an incident of unexpected drama, and to her relief the murmur of small talk which had ceased abruptly the moment they entered was resumed with increased intensity under cover of the music.

Francisco put down the wine list to regard her troubled face. "Cheer up, *amada*, the vultures wish to peck my bones, not yours."

Suddenly she felt very angry with the people around them. His proud refusal to discuss or even deny the

rumours surrounding his brother's death condemned him in their eyes as guilty. She wanted to jump up to defend him, to berate them for their blind obtuseness in refusing to see that his shock tactics were deliberate, brought about by the sense of betrayal he felt at having to explain to life-long friends what should have been obvious.

"They're fools, all of them!" she choked, thankful the fierce light above had been cut, leaving the tables lit only by the glow of small lamps that illuminated their surfaces but left their occupants bathed in half shadow.

She sensed he was smiling when he charged idly, "But you too think of me as a monster. Have you not found me cruel, heartless, and completely coldblooded?"

Hazel was glad of the anonymity of surrounding shadows that helped to hide a slip of composure he might have seized upon as weakness. Her voice was a mere thread of sound when she answered, "Yes, I have found you cruel – and heartless – but never coldblooded. Your worst actions have been committed in heat of passion and some deeds with which you've been credited have, I suspect, been shouldered without complaint as added penance to appease a conscience burdened by self-inflicted guilt. You weren't responsible for the death of Carmen's parents, I know it and so do you, so why do you allow the myth to grow? Friends are only human, they need the strength of your assurance to prop up their human weaknesses."

He drew in a sharp breath and leant forward. Outlined by the glow of the lamp his jawbone stood out

taut, and his eyebrows were black strokes uplifted in amazement. "Twice today I have been shocked by the outspoken views of mere infants, first Carmen and now you," he admitted slowly. For long seconds he stared across at her and her pulses began to throb as the current that ran between them disturbed emotions she had thought were too deeply frozen ever to be revived. But then with a shrug he jerked himself alert and placed her back in the ranks of adolescence with the humiliating command, "Tonight was chosen for enjoyment, not for concern. Come, *niña*, let's dance before your young brow becomes permanently wrinkled with worries too complex to be understood by one of your tender years."

It was very late and she was very tired when they returned home in the early hours. The house was silent as they made their way upstairs and when they stopped outside her door he kept his voice low to avoid disturbing the sleeping household. "Have you been happy this evening, *niña*?" he whispered, enclosing her waist in palms of steel. The effect of his charm was such she almost allowed her arms to steal around his neck, but remembering his past scathing indictments of childishness, she resisted, and drawing her slender frame erect, she marshalled every ounce of dignity into her reply.

"Perfectly, thank you. You must seek Carmen's advice again if ever you need guidance on ways of seeking absolution."

His hands tightened around her waist as if tempted to punish her sarcasm, but he changed his mind and instead lowered his head until a breath was all that separated his lips from hers. "A kiss," he mocked, "will prove that I'm completely forgiven!"

She hesitated; a refusal might help him guess that her heart was hammering in her breast and every nerve in her body was clamouring for his touch. She sensed he was playing on her immaturity, confident of his ability to break down her attempted indifference by sheer force of charm, but she had no intention of allowing him to guess how nearly he was succeeding. She raised her head and rested her cool young mouth upon his, projecting into the kiss passion, yearning and tenderness but still somehow retaining a hint of mystery to keep him deceived. For as long as the kiss lasted he remained startlingly still, then when she drew back he breathed in deeply and searched her face for signs of disturbance. Composedly, Hazel stared him out, suppressing a longing to throw herself in his arms and beg for the love it was not in him to give. Bitter triumph filled her when he retreated a step and with lines of tension scoring his mouth, apologized stiffly, "Forgive my teasing, *amada*. I ought to have realized sooner how completely the child has been overtaken by the woman . . ."

CHAPTER XIII

THEY returned to the Casa a few days sooner than planned because Tio Garcia found the heat of the town trying. Carmen, once the novelty of sight-seeing had worn off, admitted to a yearning for the quiet gardens and private beach of home, whereas Hazel, once Francisco's flying visit had ended, endured a great ache which she knew would only be assuaged by his company. So happily they packed their things and without bothering to inform anyone beforehand of their decision, set off on the return journey. Hazel spoke little as the car ate up the intervening miles; her thoughts were with Francisco, wondering if he would be pleased to see them, if his welcome would be one of surprised pleasure or vexed dismay.

His expression had been unreadable on the morning after their dinner engagement when she had joined him for breakfast. Courteously he had discarded his morning paper to ask her how she was feeling after her late evening, then polite conversation had ensued across a barrier of formality, the erection of which had puzzled her greatly. He had seemed determined to shun any subject pertaining in the slightest degree towards intimacy, although once when she had looked up unexpectedly she had found his attention riveted upon her mouth with a puzzled look almost as if he were debating whether its youthful freshness really had delivered a message as old as Eve the evening before. Her quick

blush had seemed to supply the answer, for he had pushed his chair back from the table and made urgent business at the factory his excuse for a hurried exit.

The towering walls of the Casa were visible long before the car turned into the drive, so that by the time it drew up at the front entrance Hazel was keyed up to a pitch with the excitement of returning to what she now regarded as home. They had passed Francisco's car parked in the drive, so after a quick wash and a change of clothing she and Carmen went in search of him. It was a shock to find him relaxing beside the pool with Catryn stretched out on a sun-lounger next to him. She was wearing a very brief bikini, but his casual slacks and loose shirt indicated his contentment of lazing in the sunshine chatting to his attractive companion while they sipped long, cool drinks from tall, frosted glasses. His obvious surprise at the sound of their approaching footsteps blended with Catryn's frown of annoyance to make Hazel feel they were unwanted intruders.

"We're home, Tio Francisco!" Carmen greeted him gleefully, running eagerly into arms which she last remembered as kind. "We missed you so," she hugged him, "we had such fun that day on your boat we've talked of nothing else since! Hazel says that perhaps some day you'll take us again, when you have time, so if you do will you teach me now to hold the wheel? I promise not to be afraid, especially if you hold me as tightly as you held Hazel!"

Catryn's eyes raked like claws across Hazel's crimson cheeks, making it an effort to remember that she was Francisco's wife, with every right to share his leisure,

as she faced the fury of a woman who, of necessity, must have received plenty of attention to warrant such a display of jealousy.

"Come along, Carmen," she urged, hot with embarrassment, "your uncle is busy just now, you can talk to him later." But Carmen had no intention of being prised away, she tightened her arms around her uncle's neck and made no bones about her preference for his company as she pleaded:

"Please, Tio, let me stay so that we can talk some more about the lady who was unkind to you, I've thought of another idea which might help to make her like you!"

When her uncle burst out laughing she knew she had won, but only a partial victory, as was made plain when he sat down and lifted her on to his knee. "We'll leave our private discussions until later, if you don't mind, *niña*, otherwise we might bore our guest." Even beauty such as Catryn's can be rendered ugly with anger; in the space of seconds she was relegated from the favoured position of companion to the dubious rating of a mere guest. She jumped to her feet, turning her back so Francisco could no longer see her face, and vented her fury on Hazel by shafting her a look of hard dislike before plunging into the pool with a splash deliberately calculated to shower water all over her. Hazel gasped at the unexpected sting of cold water against her bare arms and when Carmen cried out in sympathy she reacted by spinning round to face her and her uncle, only to be piqued beyond endurance at the sight of Francisco's broad grin. Huffily, she tossed her head and stalked off to change her sodden dress.

Catryn sought her out later that evening. After a mere apology of a knock, she stalked uninvited into Hazel's room just as she was dressing for dinner. She was hesitating over a new gown chosen from the collection sent from Madrid. The bodice was just two broad strips of material attached to the waistband to travel upwards across her shoulders and down until they reached and were caught up in the waistband at the back. At first glance it looked fairly demure, a sheath of figure-hugging jersey, gossamer light, shaded from deep rose to tender pink. But the daring cleavage was worrying. Her eyes reflected doubt as she turned from the mirror to face Catryn's advancing figure. "My word, the butterfly is certainly spreading her wings!" she greeted Hazel, her derogatory stare just failing to conceal chargin.

"Is there something I can do for you?" Hazel enquired, her tone and expression distant. Catryn, she was certain, had come to gloat, to make clear that the attachment existing between herself and Francisco had not gone unnoticed, so she drew herself erect and waited proudly for the stab of cutting words. But much to her surprise Catryn's initial remark lacked bite. Perhaps her own new-found maturity was responsible, but it was as if the sting had been withdrawn from a jab which once would have left her quivering.

"Oh, really, Nut-brown, don't assume a *marquesa's* airs with me – under that façade of assurance you're still little Miss Nobody and always will be!"

Her watchful eyes widened when a dimple appeared at the corner of Hazel's mouth and dimly she became aware of armour deflecting arrows of spite away from

the poised woman who had suddenly arisen from the ashes of a timid, uncertain girl. Fury erupted as she sought and found the reason for the change. "So," she charged softly, "you think your position impregnable? Because of a few interludes shared with a man too courteous to betray boredom you have begun weaving stupid dreams around his unsuspecting head! Well, let me put you wise, Nut-brown! Francisco is not for you. He married you to provide a playmate for his niece and if he'd combed the world he couldn't have found one more suitable – someone old enough in years to comply with the demands of convention but physically, mentally and emotionally a complete infant!" She drew in a triumphant breath and took stock of Hazel's stricken face; her shaft had driven straight through the enemy's defences.

"That's not true!" she clenched, clinging to tattered pride, unwilling to believe Francisco could have confided in Catryn the reasons behind their marriage, especially when he had made his displeasure so obvious the night he had accused her of the same transgression.

"Isn't it?" Catryn allowed a vicious smile. "I think you know it is. Believe me, my dear," she patronized, "it's much better that you face facts. Francisco must take part of the blame for your disastrous alliance, but surely he can be excused if you consider what his state of mind must have been to even consider such a drastic step. Anyway, I can't see you losing on the deal; he's sure to settle a goodly sum on you as alimony."

"Alimony?" Hazel repeated, confused by the reference.

"Surely. Knowing Francisco, he'll insist upon pro-

viding for you even after the divorce."

"There'll be no divorce," Hazel contradicted, her heart soaring at this proof that Catryn's statement was mere fabrication. "On that subject he has always been most adamant. Broken marriages are unknown in the Drach family, but besides his own personal feelings he has to consider his duty to his position. Even in these enlightened days divorce is a dirty word to the *aristocracia* of Spain!" Catryn stared, her mind too attuned to the permissiveness of modern society to cope immediately with such an outmoded viewpoint. But the serenity of Hazel's expression was convincing enough to procure from her a thin, venomous smile. Uneasily, Hazel shifted, the masklike rigidity of Catryn's features stirring vague forebodings that had their origin in memories of past hurt inflicted by the wilful girl who all her life had schemed to have her every wish granted. Something about her eyes made Hazel shiver; they had the glazed, half-demented glitter of a fanatic – one who never had and never would admit to defeat.

Hazel's shiver seemed to act as a warning. With a tremendous effort Catryn pulled herself together and the thin smile on her lips widened as she answered obliquely, "There are more ways than one of skinning a cat!" The northern homily fell with such assurance from her lips Hazel tensed, facing with sick dismay the utter uselessness of trying to thwart whatever secret alternative had been hatched by Catryn – with Francisco's blessing.

They walked in silence down the passageway, immersed in thought, but as they approached Francisco's room his appearance on the threshold brought them

to a halt. Hazel's pulses leapt as his glance swept, physical as a touch, over her slim body, then subsided with a thump when he frowned. Against immaculate linen his tan stood out deeply brown, he looked relaxed with one hand slid negligently into the pocket of black slacks, but the sound of keys jangling in impatient fingers gave the lie to an overall impression of unconcern. As his glance lingered on the cleavage of her dress his frown deepened, giving a definite impression that at any moment he was about to order her to discard the dress for one less obvious. She stiffened; suddenly his insistence upon having his own way appeared as a threat to her personal liberty: if the command came, she decided, it would not be obeyed! When her chin tilted and a pair of defiant eyes parried his frown his surprise showed in uplifted eyebrows, but then he confused her by addressing a smooth request to Catryn.

"Would you mind making your way downstairs alone? Tio Garcia will be waiting in the salon and Hazel and I will join you both there for a drink before dinner."

Instead of showing anger, Catryn smiled, a smile of understanding, of conspiracy almost, that seemed to convey to Hazel: "Make the most of today, tomorrow is mine!"

A cold hand squeezed her heart as Catryn swept confidently towards the stairs and doubts which only minutes before had been laid were once more revived. Perhaps, after all, the conclusions Catryn had drawn had not been the result of educated guesswork; her whole manner exuded the assurance of one well informed as if she knew and approved of the words

about to pass between herself and Francisco. Divorce Hazel dismissed as impossible, but then her mind began to race, resisting like a wild thing the alternative that had once before presented itself – an annulment carried with it no shame, no dishonour to soil the tapestry of Drach history . . . !

She looked calm as she stepped past him into the room, but it was the calm of numbness, a blessed freezing of the senses which she hoped might last long enough to see her through the coming ordeal. He closed the door, then with inconsistent edginess began pacing the room. Twice he stopped, seemingly on the verge of speech, then he changed his mind and turned away. She needed no more to convince her that what he had to say was of the utmost importance, never had she seen him so utterly at a loss for words. She waited with head bowed, her hands clasped childishly behind her back so that he could not see the convulsive tightening of her fingers as tension reacted upon her nerves.

"Hazel!" he began, swinging impulsively on his heel, "there is something I must have explained. That night in Palma," she knew his keen eyes had noted her start of surprise, "I thought . . . I began to suspect . . ." he broke off and strode towards her, close enough to tip up her chin with an enquiring finger. "*Did* you experience a slight change of heart that evening?"

Hazel prayed desperately for help as she faced her inquisitor. Alone, she could not hope to hide the humiliation his words had aroused. Catryn had paved the way for his approach to the subject of an annulment, but even she had not pierced the façade of arrogance which shielded a conscience tender enough to coerce

him into guardianship of Carmen, a conscience which even now was uneasy at the thought of discarding a bride he suspected might have fallen in love with him.

From somewhere she found the strength to meet his challenge with upraised eyebrows and a scorn-tipped smile. "Hardly a change of heart," she murmured. "I'll admit to a moment of weakness that evening, but only a very slight one. After all, Francisco, a few glasses of champagne can make any woman forgetful and almost any man seem charming!"

A light was extinguished from behind his eyes; she saw its demise just before her glance dropped downwards to cling as if to a lifeline upon a monogrammed stud displayed darkly against a stark white cuff. He brooded down with mouth compressed to contain a muscle jerking spasmodically at its edge. "Are you implying you used wine as an antidote – a counter-irritant – against the loathing you felt for my company?"

But for Catryn's warning Hazel might have believed hurt was buried deep amongst his words, might even have felt pity for the man whose pride she had so obviously offended, but being forearmed, she was able to recognize such signs as false pretensions adopted purely for the sake of convention. Suddenly she felt she could not endure the verbal skirmishing a moment longer. Francisco wanted Catryn and Catryn wanted him – only an unwanted bride stood in their way . . .

"How soon can an annulment be arranged?" she blurted out, receiving small satisfaction from beating him to the subject. His head jerked up, obviously surprised that she had guessed what was in his mind, then a dark tide of colour rose under his tan, then

ebbed, leaving his face starkly unemotional, a mask of unfeeling granite. "*How soon?*" she pressed, piling self-inflicted torture upon her already overburdened emotions.

He took a long time to answer, but when he did she felt he was seeking to excuse his own behaviour. "Are you in love with Carstair?" he rasped. "Is that why you wish to be free – so that you can marry him?"

She closed her eyes to ease the agony of prickling eyelids, then because words were beyond her she nodded, dislodging tears that ran a scalding path down her cheeks. With a gentleness that wrung her heart, Francisco traced their path and caught on his fingertip a teardrop that remained trembling on her lashes. His hands slipped to her shoulders, to pull her forward, steadying her trembling body in his arms. Far above her head she heard him grate, "Whatever is in my power to give you shall have, *amada*, your future happiness is my greatest concern."

His sincerity was unbelievable, for one fleeting moment she felt it might almost be genuine . . . She was put from him as if the hands that held her found her hot to the touch and as he walked away she wondered at the dejection of the proud head. Guilt, she supposed, was the cause; if nothing else, the Marqués de Drach was ever conscious of his obligations.

He was searching in the drawer of his desk and he straightened to send her a grave smile as he approached carrying an unusually shaped container. "Carmen's idea," he explained, pushing it into her hands, "a small gift to express remorse for my unreasonable temper."

Hazel accepted the oval container, its surface showing an impression of many hands upon its covering of beige-coloured suede. A tiny gold latch invited investigation and when she prised it open he was by her side to hear her first reverent gasp.

Inside was an egg, shaped out of delicate enamel and set upon a stand of gold studded with diamonds. Decorating its surface were leaves of deep green jade enclosing stems of daisies, each starry petal a flawless white pearl, each heart a golden diamond bursting with light.

"A Fabergé easter egg," Francisco explained, "commissioned many years ago by an Emperor of Russia as a present for the Empress." Her huge wondering eyes lacked comprehension when he indicated a petal standing out fractionally from the rest, so he took her hand and guided her fingers until they rested upon the upraised pearl. "Press downward," he instructed, then allowed her to explore unaided.

Nervously she exerted pressure, almost afraid to touch the precious antique, and expelled a breath of delight when the top of the egg slid open to allow two curved branches to emerge with, on each, a tiny glass miniature frame. Carmen's merry eyes twinkled from one of the frames, but the other was empty. "The Empress chose a miniature of her husband to partner one of her eldest child," he told her dryly, leaving the blank aperture to speak for itself.

Hazel drew in a shuddering breath; the piece was so incredibly lovely that her eyes refused to be drawn from it, but the vacant space was indicative of the empty life she faced without him – not even a pictured likeness

was to help to fill the void his absence would leave in her heart.

"It must be priceless," she whispered, her lips too stiff to smile.

"It is," he agreed, watching her carefully, "but its purchase did not cost me quite all I possess – as Carmen suggested it should."

"You *bought* it? For me . . . ? But why? Surely not just to appease the whim of a child?"

"Not exactly," he hesitated, again lost for words. In that small space of time realization came. This was his way of rendering payment for her services! The money already settled upon her was enough to last her lifetime, but this gift was a bonus, a thank-you for departing from his life without fuss!

"I won't take it!" She barely recognized the hard voice as her own.

He drew back as if from a blow, then recovered with an effort that showed itself in a tightening of displeasure around a mouth that had resumed its usual arrogant tilt. When he glittered angrily she felt a bitter gladness that he had abandoned the sweet reason which had been tearing her nerves to shreds; she was used to battling with an autocratic *marqués* and although her victories had been few she felt more competent to cope with anger than with melting tenderness. But she was not prepared for the aggravated grip upon her shoulders, nor for the shaking which he prolonged until she cried out for mercy.

"You ill-tempered beast!" she flared, sweeping unkempt strands of hair from her face in order to glare golden-eyed fury at her dark avenger.

"You denied any change of heart!" he clamped, "but there has been a change, although not the one I sought. I dislike intensely your cool, distant manner — never have you been so downright unapproachable!"

Unbearably goaded, she spat back, "You are inconsistent, *señor*! First you complain about my childishness, and now you reprove me for my maturity! So sorry I grew up without your permission!" she choked on her own daring, "but whether you like it or not, Carmen is the only child at the Casa now!"

Mercilessly she was held captive and when her lips moved to continue with her tirade Francisco's head swooped down to silence her with a hard, punishing kiss. She did not resist, but neither was it possible to respond to the stamp of anger upon her mouth. He lifted his head and smiled the smile of El Diablo while he raked her slender shape with contempt. Scornfully, he flicked a casual finger along the neckline of her dress.

"Take it off, *niña*," he jeered, goaded once more into cruelty. Grim amusement showed when she shied away, and she felt like a child being reprimanded for precociousness when he put the seal upon her humiliation by decreeing, "Grown up though you profess to be, you are not yet ready to fulfil the promise this dress was designed to offer!"

CHAPTER XIV

FRANCISCO decided his business trip to Formentor could be postponed no longer, so next day he left early with Tio Garcia, who had decided to accompany him on the journey. Carmen had not been to the caves and surprisingly Catryn offered to take her. They were in the breakfast salon, lingering over a final cup of coffee while they decided what to do to fill in the suddenly empty day.

"Can we go to the Caves, Hazel?" Carmen coaxed gently, reluctant to intrude upon the privacy of one whose thoughts were obviously far away.

Hazel's brow puckered; her own visit to the caves had been made immeasurably more enjoyable because she had been in the company of only one other person, whereas visiting today would mean shuffling slowly along behind a queue of camera-happy tourists whose popping flashbulbs might spoil for ever her memories of that first enchanting visit. Reading refusal in her frown, Catryn stepped in with the suggestion.

"A party from my hotel is to tour the caves later today, and I've been commissioned to escort them. If you like, you can meet me in Porto Cristo and Carmen can join our excursion while you enjoy a wander around the shops."

It was too good an offer to refuse, but even so Hazel hesitated; Catryn extended herself only to further her own ends, and while there seemed to be no underlying

motive behind her suggestion, suspicion nagged. The decision was taken out of her hands however, when Carmen squealed, "Oh, yes, please – if I have to wait another day to see the blue lagoon I'll *die*!"

When Catryn drove back to the hotel to resume her duties the time and place of their meeting had been satisfactorily arranged. Hazel and Carmen were to pick up a bus for Porto Cristo which ran regularly along the road outside the Casa. As Catryn's party were to join the last tour of the day, late in the afternoon, Hazel decided to pack a picnic lunch and catch an early bus so that they would have plenty of time to explore the pleasant little town she had first visited with Robin. It was a hot, dusty, bus ride made enjoyable by the pleasantries of local villagers who made plain the honour they felt at having the Marqués's wife and niece sharing their ride. Carmen chatted to all and sundry, explaining in detail about the outing in store and listening avidly as tales of adventure arising around the mysterious caves were recounted by the superstitious *campesinos*. When the bus finally reached Porto Cristo they bade reluctant farewell to the friendly villagers and made their way down to the harbour where they ate their picnic lunch before idling away the hours remaining watching fishing boats jockeying for position in the crowded harbour; envying the fortunate yacht owners their enjoyment of skimming coolly across lapping blue sea, and counting the seabirds that swooped and hovered over the offerings they salvaged from the remains in their lunch basket.

They were perched on the sea wall with the bustling town square behind them when Hazel glanced across

her shoulder and saw a coach with the name of Catryn's firm emblazoned upon its sides. "Gracious," she checked her watch, "Catryn's here already! Come along, darling, we mustn't keep her waiting!" She half-smiled as she sensed the drag of Carmen's feet, guessing that given half an excuse the child would change her mind, but no protest was voiced nor encouraged and she handed her over into Catryn's charge. As she watched the small figure trailing disconsolately in the wake of a crocodile of voluble tourists Hazel almost called her back, but the temptation was overcome by a desire more powerful, one which had fought for recognition all day – a desire for solitude in which to think, to plan, and perhaps even to cry a little . . .

Slowly she made her way back to the harbour to a spot sheltered by coils of rope which would protect her from the eyes of curious passers-by. Directly in front of her, on the opposite side of the harbour, was the yacht club where Robin had taken her for lunch and down below, bobbing impatiently on the water, she recognized the boat he had borrowed to make even more perfect an already perfect day. How, she mused, had Robin reacted to Francisco's brand of wild justice? Probably in the same way she herself reacted to his arrogance – with impotent anger, despair even, knowing no one yet had ever managed to penetrate the hard shell with which he was surrounded.

Tears pricked her eyelids as she wondered how Carmen would fare under Catryn's care. Probably, she gasped back a sob, the threat of sending her to convent school which, when it had suited his purpose, he had

unscrupulously used as blackmail, would become reality once Catryn was installed at the Casa. She wanted to hate him, but she could not, not when she considered the many others who had fallen under the spell of Catryn's beauty. Since childhood she had stood in her shadow, tongue-tied by her wit, admiring of her vivacity, but frightened of the flail of her cruel tongue. Quite suddenly, there on the sea wall, she made up her mind. Carmen's happiness must not be ruined nor her childhood spoiled – with or without Francisco's permission, she would take the child with her when she left!

Some of her incredible burden of unhappiness was lifted by the decision and her steps were fractionally lighter when an hour later she made her way towards the gardens where flowers bloomed and peacocks strutted before the bemused, dazzled crowd just beginning to make its way out of the cool underworld of caverns. Hazel waited, half-smiling, expecting at any moment to hear Carmen's voice call her by name, but the crowd gradually thinned as one by one the coaches pulled away until only Catryn's was left standing, its occupants all seated, an impatient driver honking madly on the horn. With a feeling of unease, she started towards the massive wooden door which marked the exit. As she began descending the slope leading into the caves panic quickened her steps so that she was almost running when Catryn appeared out of the darkness and made to swing shut the door, obviously intending to lock it with the huge key she was holding in her hand.

"Where's Carmen?" Hazel gasped. "I've been

waiting ages and I know she hasn't passed me!"

"Are you sure?" Catryn frowned. "The little devil slipped out of my clutches when we were only halfway through, but I didn't worry because I felt sure she'd tagged along with some of the other children." When Hazel stared in horror-stricken silence she bit her lip and looked apologetic. "Look, you go inside the caves and give a shout, if she's still in there she'll come running. Meanwhile, I'll check with my party and find out whether anyone remembers seeing her. Don't worry, we'll probably find her sitting in the coach!"

Hazel did not wait to tell her what she thought of her negligence, but ran past her into the tunnel of darkness. As she stumbled forward towards the first of the illuminated caves she drew in a deep breath and prepared to call Carmen's name, then just as the first syllable was about to leave her lips a curtain of darkness descended. She swung round, riveted to the spot, when a bang reverberated through the black veil of silence, then ominous waves of warning chased up her spine as she recognized it for what it was – the crash of a huge wooden door cutting off her escape into the outside world!

For an aeon of time she stood rigid in the darkness, hoping that whoever had inadvertently locked her in would be informed of her presence and return, but there was no sound other than the steady drip of water falling from a distant height into a nearby pool, and the sigh of a chilling breeze spiralling upwards to the vaulted roof. Rustles and creaks set her quivering; they might have been made by the movements of small animals or the awakening of entombed souls.

"Don't panic," she encouraged herself aloud. "Think, girl, *think!* Have you a torch? No. Matches, then?" She grovelled in her handbag and felt enormous relief when a box yielded to her searching fingers. She was trembling so much she could barely manage to scratch one alight, but when she did she felt complete darkness was preferable to eerie shadows thrown by formations of misshapen stone. At least her feet were planted firmly in the middle of the path, that much she registered before the flame flickered and died.

Cautiously, she turned and began retracing her steps. Somewhere near the exit was the master switch; if she could find it and switch on the lights her predicament would become so much more bearable. Inch by inch she faltered her way ahead, fighting hysterical fear by reasoning aloud in firmly controlled tones, "The path should begin to rise somewhere about here, then there'll be steps — about fourteen, if I remember correctly — and after that the switch which should be about halfway up the wall to the right — no, the left, now I'm facing in an opposite direction." Sweat began trickling between her shoulder blades, progress was very slow, she ought to have reached the steps by now but the darkness was so deceiving . . .

A loose stone was dislodged by her foot and went rolling downwards in front of her. She stopped suddenly and leant against a wall, thinking furiously. If she was on an incline the stone should have rolled backward! A precious match was sacrificed to enable her to find her bearings and when its flare lit her path terror and hopelessness made mockery of attempted optimism. She was lost. Somehow, she had wandered from the

path leading towards the exit and in front of her was nothing but stone and water, caverns as ancient as time, and water which for all she knew might have begun an insidious creep upwards to a higher level. She had to exercise great control to prevent herself from screaming. Obviously what was needed was a plan of action! The temperature of the air was not very low but still low enough to cause her a chill if she sat immobile. Carefully she rummaged through her bag and found a piece of chalk Carmen had deposited there earlier. She held it lightly in her fingers and began moving slowly forward, tracing it over the surface of the wall as she passed. Some time soon someone would be bound to instigate a search, and when they did arrive it would help if they had a trail to follow.

She plodded on for what seemed miles sometimes plunging into invisible puddles of water, sometimes bumping into sharp pins and spires of rock, and occasionally descending to depths where even the atmosphere felt strange. But she forged on, hoping that ahead there might be an opening leading into blessed freedom, but as time passed she began to experience hunger and thirst, and a weariness so great she was finally driven to rest. There were only four matches left in the box and she used one to search for a resting place. A thrill of horror left her sweating when by its light she saw the sheen of water. The path had narrowed until it was no more than a ledge running along a wall of crumbling rock; a veer to the left would have plunged her into a pool of deep silence!

Hazel slid to the ground, too exhausted to continue further and too frightened to even pretend bravery.

How much longer before help came? Her only consolation was the fact that Carmen was obviously not in the caves, she must have slipped past unnoticed in the crowd. But she had surely been found? Why, then, hadn't Catryn returned to the caves immediately with the news? Her heart, numbed through it was, skipped a beat. What if, as a result of some dreadful misunderstanding, she were to be left in the caves all night? The water was salty, thirst had driven her into dipping a hand into the pool, but she had had to spit out the moisture licked from dripping fingers. Chill was striking through her flimsy cotton slacks and a light cardigan offered little protection for arms left bare by a sleeveless sun top. Stiffly, she moved position and winced as sharp needles of rock pierced her flesh. She had shouted until her throat rasped sore, vaguely hoping someone about might hear her calls for help, but her cries had echoed mockingly, bouncing through the caverns and reverberating against high walls, returning like boomerangs to their place of rest. She had no way of knowing if it was still daylight, twice she had lost consciousness and the blessed periods of oblivion could have lasted for hours or even days. She was in a void of darkness and time, wherein nothing seemed to matter – not even Francisco's cruel desertion. Lightheaded, she moaned, the sound so faint it barely penetrated her lips. Perhaps he would consider her accident providential, it would at least prevent scandal if instead of being publicly discarded she should obligingly die . . .

Suddenly an object hurtled out of the darkness uttering a terrifying squawk as it winged past her face. Hazel screamed – a last terror-crazed effort born of

sheer desperation – that ripped high-pitched from her throat, then subsided into a sob only seconds before she fainted . . .

She was rambling in her delirium, calling out for Francisco and hearing him answer to his name. His grip was tight around her body as he swung her up into his arms and his face when it swam into vision was as forbidding as a monster's, a profile etched in granite with eyes distracted, as if they'd looked upon hell. Fear drained from her. Even though still aware of surrounding danger she was no longer alone; Francisco was sharing her nightmare. She wanted to comfort him, but the words would not come, so only in spirit could she share the agony betrayed by a frantic ejaculation hissed through lips tight with fury. "*Por Dios!* Someone shall suffer for this *acto diabolico!*"

Like the wings of a captured bird eager to fly, yet hesitant of release, her eyelids fluttered. Cautiously she risked a peep from under lowered lashes and felt a great upsurge of relief at the sight of familiar pearl and ivory objects gracing her own bedroom. Thoughts were clamouring for admittance into her mind, but she resisted the urge to remember, sensing that the experience might be hurtful. A slight movement caught her attention and her eyes swung towards it, almost betraying her wakefulness with a soft gasp which she only just managed to suppress as she recognized Francisco. He was sitting in a chair at her bedside, his dark head resting against the upholstery, his eyes closed. Against ivory velvet his face looked drained of colour, haggard and blue-jowled, as if shaving had been a sketchy affair accomplished swiftly because he

had begrudged the time. She felt a lazy sense of guilt which did not prevent her from tracing through tears the contours of his defenceless face. For once he was at her mercy, with guard lowered, his lips denuded by sleep of their arrogant tilt, his piercing glances cloaked by a fan of dense lashes that showed dark as bruises against high cheekbones. She caught in a swift breath when he stirred, but it escaped in a surprised gasp when she saw his lips form her name. The sound, slight though it was, jerked him awake and sent his alert glance riveting upon her face.

"*Buenos dias*!" she attempted, paralysing shyness leaving her bereft of intelligence.

"*Madre mia*," he answered softly, eyebrows sweeping upwards, "for days now we have watched over you, despairing of your life – of your sanity even – yet when you awake you calmly wish me good day!" He began to laugh, softly, but with a despairing edge.

Hazel frowned, puzzled by his reaction. Obviously he must have been under some tremendous strain when release from it brought such crazy relief. Then suddenly she remembered. "Carmen! What happened to her, is she safe . . . ?

Swiftly he eased her back against the pillows. "She is perfectly safe, in fact she was never in any danger," he assured her, his mouth setting at some grim reminder.

"Then why . . . how did it all come about . . . ?" she frowned, fighting tears of weakness.

"Don't cry, *chiquita*, everything has been resolved," he calmed, his eyes devouring her small bewildered face. But the tears would not stop, not as long as he remained

nearby to punish her with soft endearments and glances that caressed.

"*Por mi vida!*" The savage exclamation torn from him was the first break in his defences. She was lifted against his heart by arms that imprisoned her within a vibrant tender circle. "*I love you!*" he swore hoarsely, with the impulsive recklessness of a man risking his destiny on one throw of the dice. "*Madre mia,* how I love you!"

She had dreamt many times of being loved by him, but conjecture had not even remotely captured the tantalizing emotions aroused by his first kiss of devotion. Tenderly his lips explored, pleading silently for response but holding fast on to control lest the timid creature in his arms should revolt against his flare of demanding passion. Taken completely by surprise, her lips quivered under his and his arms tightened, determined to retain their hold upon heady sweetness. With fierce tenderness he wooed her capitulation, swamping her doubts with a virile passion that convinced her she was being kissed as a woman, a desirable, enchanting woman, and not as an appealing child. The wonder of it bemused her. Life up until now had not been kind, but every ache of unhappiness, every bitter tear and hurtful slight was obliterated by the joy of knowing that in some incredible, unbelievable way she had become an essential part of his happiness.

Perhaps – even now her dazed senses urged caution – she was still dreaming and would waken to face again the terror of entombment! But her answer was wrung from lips despairing of response, a low, shaken plea earthshaking in its intensity. "Please, *amada,* don't ever leave me!" All doubts dispersed as she surrendered,

revelling in the increasing fervency of his touch, questioning nothing, not even her own wanton desire to fulfil to perfection his loving demands.

It was long afterwards, when heat of passion had been controlled to a pulsating throb, that she cradled his gaunt, emotion-ravaged face in her hands and began hesitantly to probe, "How long have you loved me, my darling?"

Gravity reflected in his dark eyes as he supplied with certainty, "How long, *carina?* I think perhaps since the day I turned a crooked corner and found Carmen playing with a solemn little creature whose golden eyes seemed to plead with me to be kind. I suspected then that you were a thief," he teased gently, delaying long enough to brush the lashes of her wide-open eyes with his lips before continuing intently, "but it was on our wedding day, when I vowed to love and to cherish you till death, that I realized how completely you had stolen my heart."

His admission removed her only remaining worry, and the happiness of knowing both sets of vows had been spoken with honesty gave to her eyes the glow of amber. "Then ours really was a marriage of love, Francisco!" she whispered.

They shared a kiss which threatened to escalate beyond the bounds of mutual thanksgiving into the realms of forgetfulness but, as if determined to eliminate all possible misunderstanding, he hung on to sanity long enough to confess, "No man ever made more drastic mistakes than I in my eagerness to keep you by my side, *carestia*. At first I reasoned that to remain on the footing of servant and employer would create breathing

space with which to win your confidence. Then, when that did not work, fear of losing you forced me to resort to deception, ruthlessness and even blackmail before the wisdom of a child pointed out the virtues of consideration and kindness. But by that time you had become completely alienated. Right before my eyes the child I had treated so badly blossomed into a woman, with a woman's instinctive knowledge of how to parry with cool indifference my every abortive attempt towards conciliation." He tipped up her chin to plead, "You know now how best to punish, *cara*, but please, I beg of you, don't exercise that power too often . . ."

Impulsively, Hazel raised her lips to his and felt him quiver under her kiss. "You'll never be hurt again, my darling," she promised earnestly, "not as you have been hurt in the past." She was thinking of Carmen's mother, of the agony he had suffered at her hands, and the thought brought pain as well as compassion to twist her heart.

Nimble thought can jump both sea and land.

It was astonishing how easily he read her mind. "Carmen's mother was very beautiful," he told her deliberately, "but as a woman she lacked the qualities of warmth and sincerity a man seeks in a wife. When I tried to extricate myself from the relationship she threatened to marry my brother, who had made no secret of his infatuation. Naturally I tried to warn him against being used as a weapon of spite, but my protests were regarded by everyone as the jealous ramblings of a rejected suitor – even by Tio Garcia, who should have known me better." His jaw tautened at the memory, but he forced himself to continue.

"Of course, the marriage was a disaster and I felt bitterly to blame, but I tried to salve my conscience by supplying their never-ending demands for money. Finally, I reached the conclusion that perhaps they needed to stand on their own feet, that far from helping them, easy money was impeding their progress towards maturity and towards their understanding of the responsibilities they owed to their child. When I informed them of my decision," he blanched before her eyes, "they left the Casa in a rage and a few minutes later they were both dead."

He released her and moved away, his shoulders tense, squared to accept her condemnation. Forgetting her weak state completely, she threw back the bed covers to run towards him and was mere inches away when he swung round and caught her in his arms just seconds before she fell. With loving anger he swung her high against his heart and carried her across to the bed, but melting tenderness drowned all other emotions when she lifted her hand to stroke his cheeks and to assure him with concern, "I love you so, Francisco!" She was folded into his arms and kissed with a reverence that betrayed compunction at having subjected her to such emotional strain, but his expression of relief told of tremendous uplift.

"Thank you, *mia cara*," he whispered, "I thought never to hear you say those wonderful words!"

A soft knock on the door preceded Tio Garcia, who stepped aside to allow the doctor to enter the room. They faltered on the threshold, staring at the girl being thoroughly kissed by a man who, it seemed, had no intention of ever letting her go. A grin split Tio

Garcia's face. "Heaven be praised!" he whooped, startling his smiling companion, "I feel your services won't be required much longer, doctor, if as is said, love is the most healing medicine of all!"

Francisco was chased to his room to catch up on sleep he had lost during two days of solitary watch at her bedside. "He would allow no one near, with the exception of the doctor," Tio Garcia explained. "Never have I seen a man so demented the night you went missing, and when he found you . . . ! *Por mi vida!* never again do I wish to see such an expression of agony! He thought you were dying, you see," he finished simply, his voice conveying a remembrance of tragedy.

With the doctor's permission, they were sitting on the balcony of her room enjoying the sunshine. Carmen had been allowed a short visit only, but she was playing below on her swing within sight and near enough to yell fond remarks every now and then to the invalid.

"What really happened that afternoon, Tio Garcia?" she urged quietly. "Was Carmen lost, or had she slipped past me in the crowd?"

"She never went into the caves at all," he told her after a slight pause. "It seems she changed her mind and decided to rejoin you — after seeking Catryn's permission, of course," he stressed deliberately. Her hands clenched in her lap, but her expression did not change as she insisted in a low voice, "Go on . . ."

"There's not much more to say," his jaw hardened, "except that when they couldn't find you Catryn told Carmen to wait in a nearby café until the excursion

was over when, she said, you were sure to turn up to fetch her."

"But why didn't Catryn tell me this instead of sending me back into the caves . . . ?" When she stopped short, eyes wide with horror, he nodded.

"Yes, *cara*, you've guessed correctly! She locked you in deliberately, probably hoping you'd meet with an accident which would have given her a heaven-sent opportunity of consoling Francisco."

"She admitted all this?" she faltered, not wanting to believe Catryn capable of such a deed.

"Under considerable duress," Tio Garcia confessed. "Francisco can be extremely ruthless when his sanity is at stake."

"I see," she nodded, not really wanting to hear more. But with relish he carried on to outline the events of the day.

"We returned from Formentor just after seven to find Carmen in tears and Catryn waiting quite self-possessed to tell us you were missing. Of course, Francisco was not long in pointing out that her tale and Carmen's were oddly conflicting, but she was all prepared to brazen it out until he sent Carmen out of the room and concentrated with deadly menace upon getting at the truth. It was less than an hour before she broke down and admitted where you were, but he did not wait to condemn her, he rushed out of the Casa like a madman, and I can't help feeling relieved that she left the island on the first available flight, because if she had still been here when he carried you home, half-frozen and delirious with fear, he'd have murdered her without the least compunction."

Francisco was awake; Hazel had heard him splashing about under the shower earlier and now the sound of drawers sliding open and shut evidenced his presence in the next room. It was very late, so he would hardly be dressing to go out, but as he had slept for hours he was probably completely refreshed. She couldn't sleep either. She felt keyed up; the weariness that had affected her had vanished completely, to be replaced by alert expectancy and alternating feelings of yearning and fear. Fear, it seemed, played an integral part in her relationship with the man who, even now, she barely dared accept as a husband. Fear of his anger, fear of an attraction so strong she would have found death preferable to banishment, and now fear of being found wanting by a man whose eyes had mirrored reluctance when he left her to replenish a body drained to exhaustion by hours of tormented vigilance. How many other Drach brides had waited in this room bedevilled by similar doubts? She drew consolation from the costly objects around her – the men of Drach bestowed beauty in abundance upon those they loved . . .

She was standing at the window when he entered, a slight, ethereal figure clad in a negligée delicate enough to have been woven from moonbeams. She did not stir, but waited until he joined her, then when she felt his arms stealing gently around her waist she leant back until her head was resting upon his muscular chest left bare above the belted waist of a silken dressing gown.

Deliberately, he brushed aside the coil of hair from the nape of her neck and pressed cool lips to the tendrils left curling against soft skin. "*Bienquista!*" he murmured

hoarsely, "*dearly beloved!*"

Hazel spun round to press her cheek against his heart and saw moonlight caress the pearl glistening in his palm. Silently, he lifted her hand and slid the Ring of Chastity upon her finger, before pulling her close to set his seal of possession against her waiting lips. No words were needed and none exchanged; she felt she had come home after a long and weary exile. As he swooped to carry her like a piece of plunder towards the bed she heard a deep-throated growl and felt immediately unafraid, recognizing a sound known only to the cherished and much beloved brides of Drach – the sound of a dragon *purring!*

have you heard about Harlequin's great new series

Harlequin Presents

*ANNE HAMPSON
*ANNE MATHER
*VIOLET WINSPEAR

These three very popular Harlequin authors have written many outstanding romances which we have not been able to include in the regular Harlequin Series.

Now we have made special arrangements to publish many of these delightful never — before — available stories in a new author series, called "Harlequin Presents".

See following page for complete listing of titles available.

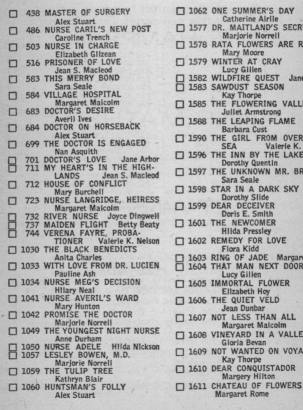

OTHER
Harlequin Romances
by MARGARET ROME

Many of these titles are available at your local bookseller,
or through the Harlequin Reader Service.

For a free catalogue listing all available Harlequin Romances,
send your name and address to:

HARLEQUIN READER SERVICE,
M.P.O. Box 707, Niagara Falls, N.Y 14302
Canadian address: Stratford, Ontario, Canada.

or use order coupon at back of book.

A
Harlequin
Romance